All Of My Nights

By

Elizabeth Castle

Name: Castle, Elizabeth, author

Title: All Of My Nights, 2021

Description: Series: All Of Me

Publishing History: China Rose, 2019

Publisher: In The Air Publishing

Identifiers: ISBN 9781967731107 (ebook) | ISBN 9781967731114 (paperback) | ISBN 9798304883894 (amazon hardcover)

Cover Designer: betibup33

Chapter One

Bo Lee watched the woman and the young girl as they crossed the street to go into the building that housed the town's grocery store, post office, and bank. He hoped her next stop would be the diner he was sitting in. It was always better when your quarry came to you. It was less likely they would suspect anything was going on, or that the meeting was orchestrated. The problem was his quarry had been elusive, always going in the opposite direction of the way he wanted her to go. He had been in town almost a week. He had socialized with several of the town's patrons, hoping word would spread.

He figured he had a couple of options. He could wait and see if she would finally take notice and seek him out on her own. Or he could approach her. It was looking like his best bet was option two, despite his preference. He was not the patient type, and he had already spent months locating her after running into one dead end after another.

Bo continued drinking his coffee while he waited for his lunch to be delivered, but his attention was on Emma. Bo kept his eyes on her until she was out of sight. She was on the small side, maybe all of five foot two. He was five-ten, something that had bothered his six-foot-three father, but still, he was much bigger than she was. She had what would probably be dark blonde hair, except it was bleached from hours under the sun. Her skin was pale despite the time she spent outdoors, and her body was toned from physical labor.

Miss Emma was a farmer, or at least she had been. Times were tough, or so he had heard from several of the other farmers and ranchers in the remote parts of Texas where he now sat. Rumors around town were that Emma would soon be losing her farm to the bank, a fairly common occurrence these days, or at least that was what he had been told.

He could feel some sympathy for her, though he found it difficult to strum up much. Life was hard for a lot of people. Emma McKinnon was just one of many who had landed on hard times. Bo was responsible for the well-being of a few hundred people, so his sympathies lay elsewhere. But right now, he had other problems besides those he employed thousands of miles away.

A few minutes later, Emma emerged from the grocery store and looked as if she were headed toward the restaurant where he sat. His gaze went from her curvy frame covered by a windbreaker to focus on the young girl. A DNA test would prove one way or the other if she was the one he was looking for, but all the evidence he had accumulated told him she was. And some part of him, deep down inside, recognized her for who she was.

He could tell the pair struck most people in town as odd: the young Caucasian woman with a petite Chinese girl at her side. He had been fielding a similar look from people since he arrived. Some looks were simply because he was a curiosity. Other looks were because the person glaring at him did not want a foreigner living in their town. But everyone he had spoken to had been surprisingly closed-mouthed about the Chinese girl living in their midst. The townsfolk had been open and full of information about Emma, but not about the little girl named Fan. He was surprised her adoptive mother had not changed her name to something more American.

Bo averted his gaze when Emma and Fan entered the restaurant. From the corner of his eye, he could see she was looking at him but seemed a bit undecided if she should come over. Then he watched as she squared her shoulders and headed his way.

"Mr. Lee?" Emma's soft voice was barely heard over the loud conversations in the restaurant.

"Yes?" Bo kept his face and tone neutral as if the meeting had not been inevitable, as if he did not know who she was.

"I'm sorry to bother you while you're having lunch, but Sheriff Lockwood said you might be interested in renting the cabin that's on my property." Emma looked down into the face of the man seated at the booth in the corner.

"I take it you are Emma McKinnon." He held out a hand to her.

Relieved that the conversation wasn't going to turn awkward, she shook the hand he held out to her. "Yes, I'm Emma. He mentioned to me that you were looking for a temporary place to stay."

Bo waved to the seat across from him. "Yes, I am.

Sheriff Lockwood said he would put out some feelers for me."

Emma picked up the girl and set her in the booth and took a seat next to her. "The cabin isn't anything fancy, but it should suit your needs. If you'd like, you can come out and see it."

The waitress, a busty woman named Linda, set a plate of food in front of Bo. "Hi there, Miss Emma. And hi there, Miss Fan. Can I get you gals anything?"

Emma was going to politely decline when Fan tugged on her jacket.

"Auntie Emma, can I get a grilled cheese?" Fan looked up at her aunt.

Bo made the decision for her. "The little lady will have a grilled cheese. How about you, Miss McKinnon?"

Emma looked down at Fan, who was grinning at the man across from them. "I wasn't planning to stay and eat. I just wanted to invite you out to see the cabin."

"We should get to know one another first. I am a stranger, after all."

Emma was torn. She didn't want to be rude, but she really couldn't afford to eat out. She only had a few dollars in her purse, and her bank account was dwindling fast. She supposed he had a point about getting to know him better, but still, she couldn't afford to stay and eat. "Sheriff Lockwood wouldn't have recommended you to me if he didn't think you were the right tenant. And since you're a new police officer here in town, I'm sure your background check was thorough."

Bo ignored her comment. "Two grilled cheese

sandwiches then for the ladies."

Emma frowned but decided not to kick up a fuss. Little Fan bounced in her seat, excited by the now-promised sandwich.

Emma declined coffee when offered but ordered a glass of milk for Fan. She tugged the lightweight jacket off the small girl and pulled out a notebook and some crayons from her oversized purse for her to play with.

Bo leaned back in his seat. "This is your niece?"

Emma shrugged out of her jacket, the warmth in the restaurant making her a little lightheaded. It was too early in the year for air conditioning but too warm for the heater to be running, and the heat from the kitchen was making the restaurant a little too warm. "Yes. She's staying with me for a while. This is Fan."

"Mommy is away. I can draw you a picture." Fan began drawing a stick figure with curly yellow hair.

Bo held out a hand to the girl. "It is nice to meet you, Fan."

The little girl giggled and shook the offered hand.

Emma brushed back the girl's long black hair and focused back on the man. "Anyway, the sheriff mentioned he'd just hired you on, and that you weren't too keen on staying at the local inn. I have the cabin, but I'll be moving in the next couple of months. But if you like the place, we can write up a contract. The new property owners will probably be happy to have a paying tenant for the old cabin."

"The sheriff mentioned you were selling." He knew the property was being foreclosed on but feigned ignorance.

Emma took a sip of the water the waitress had set in front of her to wet her dry throat. The bank was in the process of finalizing the foreclosure papers, and she wanted to cry every time she thought of it. "Not exactly. The bank will be selling it. But there is the main house and acres of property. That is what a new owner will be more concerned about. But how about you? Why here? It's a small town, not much to it, really."

"I felt like I needed a change. Is that not why most people end up in a small town?"

Emma didn't know; she'd lived here her whole life. But his accent was thick, and she highly doubted he was born in America. He didn't sound like he'd been here very long, either. But she supposed the wilds of Texas would be considered a change for most people, no matter where they were from.

Fan finished her drawing and held it up. "See. That's my Auntie Emma, and that's my mommy. This is you. You look like my daddy."

Emma was startled by the abrupt statement from the young girl. It was rare that she mentioned her father. And other than both men being Asian, nothing about the man seated across from her reminded her of Fan's father. This man was well-dressed, well-mannered, and, given the fact that he was a police officer, a man who upheld the laws instead of breaking them.

"Fan is a Chinese name. I am Chinese too."

Emma hadn't wanted to ask him but was glad he brought it up. "Fan's father is Chinese. My cousin Maryanne married Fan's father and adopted Fan."

Bo leaned back in his seat. "My mother is Chinese, and my father was American."

Emma relaxed at the change of topic, unaware of the tension in her body from the mention of Fan's father. "So you're a U.S. citizen?"

Bo nodded but did not elaborate. The waitress came and delivered two plates of grilled cheese and fries. He had learned quickly that almost every food was served with fries. He was still getting used to American food.

Fan quickly demolished half of her sandwich.

Emma took a couple of bites of hers. "Grilled cheese is her favorite. She asks for it for lunch every day."

"Always willing to oblige a lady."

Emma got the conversation back on track. "Anyway, if you are interested, I can write the directions down so you can come look at the cabin. It isn't much, but it has electricity, an electric heater, a window air conditioner, and hot water. My driveway is paved and lets out onto the main county road. My father was the town's doctor, so the county helped pay for the paving years ago. In an emergency, you won't have to worry about being stranded if the drive washes out."

"Sheriff Lockwood said the place would be exactly what I was looking for. How about I follow you home and check it out this afternoon? As lovely as the inn I am staying at is, I prefer privacy."

Emma nodded and ate a couple of fries. He didn't seem terribly interested in the plate of steak and eggs in front of him, seeming to prefer the coffee. Unable to stem her curiosity, she spoke again after finishing half the sandwich.

"How long have you been a police officer?"

Bo took a bite of his rubbery steak, then set his fork down. "Over ten years."

When Bo didn't elaborate, she dropped silent again.

Bo knew he should say something else, but his words eluded him. He was too busy studying the translucence of her skin and the delicate length of her fingers that held the sandwich. He took his gaze off her and went back to studying the child. Like him, she looked Chinese. His half-brother, Jonas, looked more American than Chinese. Though they shared the same parents, Jonas was the one who favored their father.

When the waitress returned to their table, Emma asked for a box for their food. She turned her gaze back to Bo. He was a handsome man. He smiled easily, his teeth were straight, and life and vitality shone in his eyes. But his eyes, now that she had gotten a better look, were not just brown but had flecks of green in them. They were unusual eyes. His face spoke of his heritage, his skin bronzed and his hair black. And if his skin tone and the shape of his eyes that spoke to his Chinese heritage weren't enough to cause him to stand out in the mostly Caucasian restaurant, his hair would. Its thick black mass was tied back in a braid that fell to the middle of his shoulder blades. She guessed more than a few people might have mistaken him for Native American or Hispanic from the back. But his face told a different story.

"Not hungry?" Bo watched as Emma boxed up more than half of the food on her plate. She also boxed up the remains of Fan's fries.

Emma flushed. She wasn't going to tell this man that this impromptu meal would be their dinner. She supposed she shouldn't be ashamed of the fact that she was flat broke, but she couldn't help but feel embarrassed. She was still reeling from all that had happened the past year, and she wasn't ready yet to discuss it with anyone, and certainly not a stranger. But the income from renting the cabin would go a long way to help secure her uncertain future.

"I had a big breakfast. Are you done?"

"Yes." The first thing he planned to do once settled into her cabin was to get some groceries and see what he could do to supplement his kitchen with something from home.

Emma took the extra container the waitress brought and boxed up the remainder of his food for him. She looked up at him through her lashes. "I hate to see food go to waste."

Bo nodded and set the container next to hers. "Then you take it. I will not eat it."

Emma helped Fan get her coat back on while they waited for the check. When he took her ticket, she protested. "I can pay for that."

Bo raised an eyebrow. "Since I had to coerce you into joining me for lunch, it is the least I can do. Do not worry about it. I can pay for it, too."

Emma wasn't sure that a new police officer in a town this size would get paid well, but she supposed he was probably doing a sight better than she was. She put her jacket on and then zipped Fan's. The six-year-old protested but surrendered. Fan was well-behaved, but she was still a child.

Bo pulled on his own jacket but did not bother to zip it up. "I am parked right outside. Where are you?"

"I'm across the street. See the large white truck?"

Bo nodded. "Yes. I will be right behind you."

Emma was still fastening Fan's car seat when Bo, in a large black SUV, pulled up behind her and waited patiently for her. She was grateful that the old truck had a backseat for Fan and that the truck still ran, considering it was almost as old as she was. She backed out of her parking spot and headed toward the county road she lived on.

Emma kept her fingers crossed the entire way that Bo Lee would take the cabin. It wasn't as if the town were full of newcomers. Bo was probably the first new face in years, with the exception of Fan and the children of the townsfolk. And what a face it was. Emma's heart was still racing a bit. It had been years since a man had caught her interest. There were a few men in the area who would be more than happy to make her a Mrs., but she wasn't interested. She had been engaged at nineteen, and that relationship had taught her everything she cared to know. She had dated a few times over the years, but none of those men made her change her mind about commitment and marriage.

But Bo Lee definitely set off a few of her feminine alarms. He was much taller than she was. He was lean, but his shoulders were broad, and his body wasn't what she would call skinny. And his arms, exposed by the short-sleeve shirt he wore at lunch, were thick and ropy with muscle. Give him a Stetson, and he'd pass for a cowboy. Like most women born in the country, she had a thing for cowboys.

The drive to her spread didn't take long, so she wasn't forced to keep wondering about Bo, where he came from, or how long he'd stay. She wouldn't be here any longer than a month or two. Her cousin would be coming at the end of the month, just a few short weeks away, and shortly after that, the bank would officially own her home.

Emma pulled up in front of the cabin. The main house was visible from the cabin, and in comparison, the cabin looked old and worn. She climbed out of the truck and helped Fan from the car seat. Fan clasped her arms around her neck, a sure sign she wasn't ready to be put down yet. Emma hiked the girl to her hip and crossed to where Bo was waiting.

Emma handed him the keys. "Here. It's not much, but it's been kept up over the years. I clean the dust out regularly, and I can guarantee there aren't any critters living inside."

Bo took the keys and unlocked the cabin door. "I thought most people in the country did not bother to lock their doors."

Emma followed Bo inside. "I don't suppose most do, but I'm off a main road, and I don't like to tempt people. We get a few drifters from time to time."

Bo took a look around. The cabin was not much, but like she said, it was clean. It did not smell musty, and the furniture looked fairly comfortable. There was a twin bed tucked in the corner, and a bath off to the side, next to what passed for a kitchen. It did have a stove, a sink, and a full-size fridge. He could make it work, though the twin bed might have to go. Not that he had much of a choice. Living in the cabin was the easiest way to keep an eye on Emma and on anyone who might come and go.

Bo turned to look at Emma, who was waiting near the door. Fan had her head lying on the woman's shoulder, her dark brown eyes watching him. "I will take it."

Emma nodded, the knot in her stomach unraveling. "Great. I have some linens and some other stuff up at the main house I can bring over for you when you're ready to move in."

Bo glanced around. "I am ready now. I just have to get my things from the inn. I did not bring much with me."

Emma went outside and set Fan down. Fan went racing toward the main house. Knowing the little girl would head straight for her toys, she turned back to Bo. "I'll get some towels and sheets, and I have a quilt. It can get chilly in the evenings this time of year. There is also wood stacked and covered behind the cabin if you prefer a fire to the electric heater."

Bo started walking back to his SUV while Emma trailed behind him. "I will be back in a couple of hours. I need to stop in at the station as well. Will everything be set by then?"

Emma stepped to the side when Bo opened the door to his vehicle and climbed inside. "I can have everything together before you get back."

"Have the lease ready, and I will stop by the main house to sign it."

Emma nodded again. She remained where she was until Bo was gone. Once he was no longer in view, she drove to the main house. It only took a few minutes to gather the linens and the few necessities he would need. She loaded up the truck and then went to grab a few food items. She doubted he'd have time to shop, and he had bought them lunch.

An hour later, the cabin was ready, and Emma was back home. She glanced out the window, up at the gray sky. A winter storm was coming. It hurt to know that this winter would be her last one here in her family home. And it hurt that she wouldn't be around to watch the spring planting. But Bo, whether he knew it or not, was a godsend. His money, though it wasn't much, was going to provide the nest egg she needed to make a new life for herself. She just had to figure out what that life looked like.

Emma glanced over at Fan, who was playing with her dolls. Maryanne, Fan's mother, would be back soon. Maryanne was already making plans for her and Fan when she returned, plans that would take them away from Texas. Emma sighed and went back to the kitchen to wash up the day's dishes.

Emma brushed the tears that wet her cheeks. She missed her cousin, missed her mother, and missed her father. And soon, she'd learn what it felt like to miss her home. Straightening her spine, Emma scrubbed the dishes and then went to play with Fan. Her future might be unknown, but she would survive. That's what McKinnons did.

Chapter Two

"I heard you met Miss Emma today." Sheriff Martin Lockwood shifted his weight in the chair behind his desk as he watched his new officer enter the room. The police station was too small to hold any offices, so his desk was tucked away from the front desk, but still in the same room. He liked being able to watch people come and go.

Bo took a seat behind his desk and booted up the ancient computer, not at all surprised that the sheriff knew of his meeting with Emma today. "I did. I have decided to take the cabin. It is remote enough to give me the breathing space I want, but close enough to town in case I am needed in a hurry."

Martin nodded at that but otherwise didn't move. "It will be nice for her to have someone around to keep an eye on things. She had some trouble a couple of months ago. Well, it was her cousin who had the trouble, and she brought it with her."

Bo had not heard the tale, though he knew from police reports the facts. A man named Ping Biao had shown up on the homestead, beat the cousin within an inch of her life, and disappeared when Emma had pulled a shotgun out and charged the man with it. Biao had not liked the fact that his wife and daughter had disappeared, and he had easily tracked them down. But as far as the report stated, he had not been back.

Bo was more interested in what the reports had not said, but the officers had been closed-mouthed about the incident, much as the townsfolk had been about Fan.

Bo shifted the chair so he could look Martin in the eyes. "Has anyone seen or heard from him since he left?"

"No. Most people in town never laid eyes on him at all. No one has seen him since then either, and believe me, a Chinese man in the middle of town would have stuck out had he made his way through. If you ask Emma, she'll say she hasn't seen him since. My concern is that she might lie if she thinks it will protect her cousin. She didn't want me digging into this Ping character. She said it was too dangerous."

Bo digested that tidbit. He was fairly certain Emma was not aware of what was really going on with Biao. He imagined she had some suspicions about him, and those suspicions would keep her from wanting to involve anyone else. Bo had no doubts the cousin knew exactly who and what her husband was. The woman would have had to be blind and completely naive not to know her husband was a criminal. But he could very well imagine that Maryanne Biao would have kept her secrets from her cousin to protect her.

Bo thought back to Martin's comment that Emma said it was too dangerous to go digging into Biao's past. "I do not suppose that stopped you."

"Nope. The problem was not that much information came up when I tried to find out more about him. When I tried to dig further, I got an immediate response to back off from the FBI, right after they grilled me. And then I got you."

"And then you got me." Very few people knew why Bo was in this part of the country. His brother Jonas, who worked for the FBI, might still be on the hunt for Biao, but as far as Bo was concerned, his own duty was done. He had fulfilled the obligations he felt he had to both his country and his family. His mission here was strictly personal. But he was grateful to his friends and family for backing him up. And a little help from a new friend in the CIA had not hurt either. Griffith Dunn was retired but still had a lot of connections. He just happened to know a man who knew a man who knew Martin Lockwood. Bo did not ask too many questions, and Griffith did not offer much in the way of explanations.

Martin Lockwood had not been terribly happy to find Bo in his office a couple of weeks ago. Bo could not blame the man. The sheriff was worried Bo would bring trouble to his quiet town. Bo had calmly reminded him that trouble had already found his town, and should that trouble return, Bo was more than equipped to handle the situation. Bo had promised to keep a low profile and to disturb the town as little as possible. Martin had offered him temporary employment, which helped explain to the townsfolk why a stranger, and a Chinese one at that, had come to their small town.

Martin spoke after Bo had dropped silent. "What are you going to tell Emma?"

"Nothing. I trust your judgment, and if you think she

would not tell you anything, then the likelihood of her telling me is slim. Plus, there really is no evidence that Biao will return. And considering he has a daughter and not a son, his return is even less likely."

"You think a girl is not worth his trouble?" Martin considered the man's words.

"If he had a son, he would want him to follow in his footsteps. The fact that he has a daughter and let his wife legally adopt her tells me his interest in his daughter is slim at best. He can dump his daughter on his wife and forget all about her."

Martin wasn't sure he bought Bo's theory. "Then why did he come back for her?"

Bo shook his head. "He did not come back for Fan. I do not know what his reasons were. But he beat his wife, most likely trying to get information out of her. If his interest was in Fan, he could have easily overpowered both women, despite the shotgun, grabbed the girl, and disappeared."

"True enough. You should head back over there and get settled. Nothing is likely to happen around here on a Wednesday night." Martin waved Bo off.

Bo turned his back to the sheriff and smiled. Nothing was likely to happen tonight, or tomorrow night, or any other night. The closest thing to trouble this town had was when the men who got a little lively on Friday and Saturday nights at the town's two local bars got into a fight. One bar was for the normal crowd, those who just wanted to get out and have a good time. The other one was for the hard-core drinkers, those who were not interested in live music or getting away from the kids. It was those men, bent on drinking their problems away, who caused the most trouble.

Martin leaned forward in his seat, his face serious. "At the end of all this, there is one thing I want you to do if you catch this Biao character."

"What is that?"

Martin nodded. "Maryanne won't testify against Biao. Even when she lay bloodied in Emma's yard, she claimed nothing happened. My guess is that she is so afraid of her husband that she will never speak out. I want you to convince Emma to testify. She witnessed the attack. She gave a statement after her cousin was taken away, but a couple of days later, she was suspiciously quiet on the subject. No one comes into my town and roughs up my citizens. I know you've got bigger things for this Biao character, though you've been vague on what that is exactly, but I want him prosecuted for what he did."

Bo considered that. Since he was not actively looking for Biao anyway, making a promise to charge him did not hurt, but Bo did not really want to get involved at all. "If I do find Biao, the charges against him will keep him in prison for the rest of his life."

"And a few extra charges will make sure he doesn't get an early release. I don't know what he did, but I want him too."

Bo shrugged. "I cannot make promises, but if I can make that happen, I will."

That was good enough for Martin, who simply nodded back and then focused on his own work.

Bo finished up what little paperwork he needed to do

before he headed back out. All of his things were packed up in his SUV. He had hit the room at the inn first, anxious to get his stuff so he could settle in at Emma's place. The only things he had brought into his room were his clothes and a few personal necessities. Everything else he had brought with him to America had been left packed up in the back of the SUV. One thing he did not have to worry about in this town was vandals breaking into his car. He doubted anyone in town even bothered to lock their car doors.

The drive back to Emma's was a short one. He stepped out of the SUV and took a deep breath. The air was clean and smelled of the coming spring. There were a few other not-so-pleasant odors from the nearby barns, but even those smells were welcome. Bo had come to hate the confines of the city, longing for open pastures and open land. He would enjoy the reprieve while it lasted. When the time came, he would make his way back to his home and back to his other responsibilities in Hong Kong.

It did not take him very long to unload his belongings. When he came to America last year, he had traveled light. He carried in his suitcase and noticed that there were fresh linens on the bed. He walked to the bathroom and the bath had fresh towels. A quick check showed there were washrags, toilet paper, and a few basic cleaning supplies in the small cabinet over the toilet. It looked like his new landlady had thought of everything. He left the bedroom and on a small table in the space reserved for eating was a set of contracts, one for him and one for her. She had even left a pen. Smiling to himself, he scanned the documents and signed his name on the contracts. He lightly touched the letters he'd just wrote. It was always odd for him to see his name written in English. Though his father had been an American, he felt very little connection to his father's country. Of course, he had felt little connection to his father.

He folded the contracts and headed over to Emma's. It was warmer out now than it had been earlier. Behind the main house, he saw a large glass structure. He had noticed it when he had arrived earlier but had not paid much attention. It was mostly hidden, set back away from the house, but he was sure it was a greenhouse. Focusing back on the main house, he saw through her screen door that she had left her front door open. Light was shining from what looked like the living room. Emma was sitting on the floor at a low coffee table and was coloring with Fan.

He knocked on the screen, startling the pair. "I have brought the contracts over."

Emma awkwardly rose from her position on the floor, her foot asleep. She unlatched the screen and opened it. "Please come in."

Bo closed the screen door behind him, taking in the house. It was a simple room, the furnishings a little old, but it was a nice room. The sofa was oversized, a small television sat off to the side, and a braided area rug covered the scarred hardwood floors.

Bo followed Emma to the kitchen. Much like the living room, it looked a little worn but well kept. "I wanted to thank you for setting up the cabin so quickly. I do not have much in the way of linens and things."

Emma gestured for him to take a seat at the small

kitchen table. "I figured as much, and I have everything the cabin might need. Just let me know if you need anything else. Up until a couple of years ago, a cousin of mine lived there. She traveled a lot, so she wasn't around much, but she kept the cabin as her home base. Before that, my grandfather lived there. He and my father didn't get along so well, so he preferred living there instead of in the main house."

"I take it the cousin is not moving back in?"

"No. She moved out after she got married. Set off for the bright lights of the city with her new husband. She never did like the country much. Can I offer you some iced tea or some coffee?"

Bo was not a fan of the tea he had been served thus far, so he opted for coffee. "Coffee. Black, please."

Emma pulled a canister out of the cabinet and set about making a pot of coffee. Coffee was another one of the luxuries she had been foregoing lately, but she still had plenty to offer to guests, not that she had many. After the incident with her cousin's husband, she'd had plenty of visitors checking in on her, most notably Sheriff Lockwood. Even now he popped in once a week to check on her. She imagined he'd be a less frequent guest with one of his officers living next door.

Something occurred to her while her thoughts drifted to the sheriff. "I hope the sheriff isn't putting you up to taking the cabin."

Bo shook his head. "No. Why would you ask?"

Emma turned back to the cabinets and pulled out a couple of mugs. "The sheriff is a good man, but he tends to be a bit overprotective of the single women in the community. He will probably mention at some point that he pops over from time to time. It occurred to me that with you next door, I probably won't see him much."

Bo considered that. "It could be that he is protective. But it is more likely that he is interested."

"Interested in what?" Emma poured both of them a cup.

Bo could not help the slight, cynical laugh. "You."

Emma was glad that the coffee cup was set down, or she might have dropped it. "I can promise you the sheriff is not interested in me."

"Why not? You are young, you are attractive, and the sheriff is single. You just admitted you are too."

That stopped her for a moment. She didn't think of Martin Townsend as anything but the sheriff. He was an authority figure, and not really much else. She hadn't considered that he might be interested in her for more personal reasons. She supposed the sheriff wasn't a bad-looking man, and she could do worse. But because she wasn't interested, she probably wouldn't notice if he'd been flirting with her. She doubted he was; he was still pushing her to file charges against her cousin's husband. She kept telling him there was nothing to pursue. He wasn't going to come back, not so long as there wasn't a good reason to. And her cousin had begged her to drop it, for Fan's sake, if nothing else.

"I suppose you could be right, but I wouldn't bet money on it." Emma added a little sugar from the bowl on the table to her coffee.

Bo took a sip and savored it. She made her coffee nice and strong. If he drank coffee at all, he preferred it like this. What they served him at the restaurant might as well have been flavored water.

"So you said you came here for a change. In the rental contract, you have the cabin for six months, and an additional six months on top of that if you elect to stay. Like I said before, you'll have to negotiate with the new owners. The bank already has a buyer lined up. I know them very well. They own some of the adjacent property and already have a house. They may opt to rent out the main house and the cabin. I can't imagine them moving into this house when the one they have is much nicer. And last year, they put in an in-ground swimming pool. Those are not cheap."

Bo's brow rose as Emma spoke. When she came to an abrupt stop, he smiled. "I imagine they are not."

Emma blushed. "Sorry, I'm rambling. I've just been edgy. It will almost be a relief when I finally move. The stress has been getting to me."

"It cannot be easy losing your home. Where do you plan to go?"

"Probably not too far. There's a shopkeeper in town who offered me the apartment over her shop. It's small, but I don't need much space. Fan will be back with her mother by the time I move, so I don't have to worry about her. I imagine I'll see you in town sometimes."

Bo saw Emma's gaze go toward the window. From the kitchen, you could see the large greenhouse several yards from the house. "I do not suppose you can take that with you to an apartment."

Emma realized where her gaze had gone. Inside the greenhouse were her most precious possessions. "No, I don't suppose I can. Mabel said it wouldn't be a problem to keep coming out to tend my plants. But if her husband decides to level the house and the cabin next year and turn all the property into farmland, then the greenhouse will go, too. But that wouldn't be until next year. Who knows where I'll be then. Maybe I'll follow my cousin and move to the city."

Bo could not quite imagine Emma surrounded by the lights and activity of any city. She looked happy and serene surrounded by all this land. And though he did not much care about fashion, the worn jeans and flannel shirt, along with what he was sure were a pair of cowboy boots, would stick out in the city, any city.

Emma watched as Bo finished his coffee. She was reluctant to see him leave, and that would give her something to think about later that night while lying in bed, with sleep eluding her. "Can I get you another cup of coffee?"

"No, I should probably get going. I do not want to interfere with your routine."

Emma figured that was half her problem. She was tired of her routine. Tired of struggling; tired of worrying. Bo might just be one of the most intriguing men she'd met in a long time. She had dozens of questions she wanted to ask him. She found herself offering him dinner. "You probably don't have anything for dinner. I tossed some oatmeal and a few dried goods in your pantry, but that won't fill you up. It isn't any hassle to fix a little extra so you can join Fan and me."

Bo was surprised by the invitation, to say the least. Emma struck him as friendly, but not overly so, especially with a man she just met. She had been soft-spoken and nervous at the restaurant. But the invitation seemed genuine, and he had to admit he would not mind eating something not cooked in a restaurant. And she was right; he would have to drive into town for his meal. "If you are sure."

Emma gave him a shy smile. Then she realized she was practically staring at the man and rose. "I'm sure. I've got some vegetables from my garden in the deep freezer, and I swapped some flower seeds with my neighbor for some fresh chicken. I can have dinner ready in no time."

Bo simply sat at the table and let Emma work. It was pleasant to sit and watch a pretty woman fuss. And when Fan joined them with her coloring book in hand, he simply picked up a crayon and helped her color her princess picture.

Emma felt an ache near her heart watching the large man color with the small girl. This had been her dream once. She had wanted a family. She had wanted a husband who adored his children, who would come in after a hard day's work and be with them. She supposed in the dream the man wasn't Chinese, and her daughter wasn't a niece, but it was a lovely picture anyway.

What struck her in that moment was an odd sense of familiarity. Something in the way Bo tipped his head to the side, just the way Fan was, made the pair look like family.

Knowing that was silly, and knowing it was simply the fact that they shared superficial characteristics from being from the same culture, she went back to preparing their meal.

An hour later, the trio sat at the table, a simple meal before them. Emma had baked a loaf of bread yesterday, so she had added it to the roasted chicken and steamed veggies. She poured them a fresh cup of coffee and a glass of milk for Fan.

Bo took a bite and relished it. Though perhaps not the seasonings he was accustomed to, the roasted chicken was exactly what his palate had been craving. There was no heavy gravy, there was not a ton of butter drowning the food, and it was piping hot from the oven.

"Do you mind if I ask where you were born?" Emma was cutting up Fan's chicken when she asked.

"No, I do not mind. I was born in Hong Kong. I lived there until my father sent me to boarding school on the mainland when I was seven. Then when I was in high school, I went back and lived in Hong Kong with my father."

Emma couldn't imagine being a small child living away from home. "Did you like boarding school?"

Bo took a large bite and swallowed before answering her. "I liked boarding school just fine. My father wanted me to learn how to read and write inEnglish, along with Mandarin. He sent me to the best place he could find for me to do that."

"I guess I can understand that. Having an American father, he probably wanted his son to learn his language."

"That was part of it. But English is the language of

business. My father was a businessman and wanted me to follow in his footsteps. My father's Mandarin was mediocre at best. And he never learned how to read and write it."

"I imagine there is a lot of English spoken in Hong Kong."

Bo smiled. "Yes. Like any good port city, there are a whole lot of different languages spoken."

"Will you go back? I mean, you took this job here; you said you wanted a change. But it has to be hard to be away from your family and friends."

"My father passed away a couple of years ago. I do not have any other family in China or Hong Kong. I have an older brother, and he lives here in the U.S. Our mother came and is living here as well. She married an American who happens to be a friend of my brother's wife."

Emma, used to knowing everything about everyone else in her small community, perked up at hearing he had family here in the States. "That must be nice, having them both here. Do they live near here?"

Bo realized she made the assumption that he was here in Texas so he could be near his family. Hating to disillusion her, he simply nodded. Technically Texas was closer than Hong Kong, but he did not have any plans to spend time with his family. Once he was sure Fan was safe, he would hop back on a plane. His family kept trying to convince him that he should come live on the East Coast with them, but he had no intention of doing that. They were blood, but they were not family. And if he knew anything, he knew that the best thing he could do for them was to stay as far away as possible.

Emma interrupted his thoughts. "You've picked a nice community. Everyone here is very nice, and we're close-knit. Stay long enough, and it will be like you've always been here."

Not wanting to answer any more questions, he turned the tables. "What about you? Did you grow up here?"

"Yes. My family has lived right here on this land for five generations. My great-great-grandfather bought this land when he was a young man. The story goes he had inherited some money from a rich uncle. He wanted his own land, so he spent every penny on property. He had one son and left it to him. Then my great-grandfather had one son and one daughter. He left the land to his son. The daughter married a local farmer and raised a large family. My cousin Maryanne is descended from my great-great-aunt, the one who used to live in your cabin. Then my grandfather only had a daughter. He didn't want to leave the land to her, so he had hoped she would marry and have a son. Instead, she had me. When he passed, my mother inherited the property. When she passed, I inherited it. My father didn't feel like he should take the land, so he made sure it went to me."

"And your father has passed?"

Emma nodded, feeling her throat constrict. "He passed last year, fifteen months ago now."

"I am sorry. It was obviously hard. Did his death wipe you out?"

Emma started at the abrupt question. "That's bold. But no, it didn't. An older cousin who cultivates my grandfather's land had a stroke. He couldn't pay the rent on the land. And when he couldn't pay the rent, I couldn't pay the mortgage. My grandfather had taken out a mortgage to expand his operation, but in the end, he ended up renting the land to my cousin. My grandfather didn't believe that a woman could run a farm. So he let my older male cousin use his land to expand his operation instead. That's when things went bad."

"I am sorry, Emma, that was rude." Bo apologized, but he was not sorry he asked. He wanted to know.

Emma sighed. "Not really. Lots of people have been curious. I worked for my father. I ran his clinic. And when I wasn't running his clinic, I worked in my greenhouse. I suppose I have farmer's blood running through my veins, regardless of my gender. I had always hoped that my grandpa would realize that, but he was stubborn until the day he died. He never forgave my mother for marrying a doctor instead of a farmer and for having a girl instead of a boy."

"I want to be a princess." Fan piped in as she crammed a handful of green beans into her mouth.

Emma laughed and smiled at the young girl. "You can be whatever you want to be."

Bo relaxed in his seat. "It is a lofty ambition, to be sure."

Emma smiled at him. "We should all dream so big. Did you always want to be a police officer?"

Bo shook his head. "No. When I was younger, I was interested in music and martial arts. I guess I always thought I would be one or the other."

"Were you good at either one of them?"

Bo took his last bite. "I was good at both, but you know how it goes. Somehow or another, those dreams were put away, and I became a cop."

"Yes, I know how that happens. I wanted to run a nursery. Instead, I ended up as an office manager. Somehow that wasn't how I thought my life would end up."

Bo glanced out the window at the greenhouse. "What do you grow in there?"

Emma picked up their plates. "If you really want to know, stop by sometime and I'll show you."

Bo finished his coffee. "I will do that."

Emma picked up Fan and took her to the sink. She washed her face and hands. She then set her down to run off and play.

"I hope you enjoyed dinner."

"I cannot thank you enough for inviting me. I have not had a decent meal since I came here."

"Here, Texas, or here, America?"

Bo could not help but laugh at the question. "Texas. Before when I lived in more urban areas, I was able to find some stores that sold authentic Chinese fare. I will have to cook for you one day, assuming I can find something in your grocery stores."

"Grocery store, singular. But these days, with the internet, I've no doubt you can get what you want delivered."

Bo rose. "I might try that. Thank you, Emma."
"You're welcome."
Bo gave her a slight bow and excused himself.

Emma found herself following him. She stayed behind the screen door watching until he entered the cabin. Sighing, she closed the front door behind her. She found herself hoping that they might have that dinner one day.

Chapter Three

"Why is he doing that?" Fan sat on the front porch, watching Bo in the distance.

Emma answered without thinking. "He's torturing the female species."

Fan giggled. "You're silly, Auntie Emma."

Emma tore her gaze away from Bo and back to the peas she was shelling. Almost every morning for the past two weeks she'd woken up before the sun was even up all the way to find Bo outside. No doubt there was no room inside his small cabin to exercise. When Bo had mentioned he'd enjoyed music and martial arts, she hadn't realized he still practiced the martial arts part. But every morning he was outside, wearing nothing more than a loose pair of pants, his body glistening with sweat as he put his body through a series of exercises.

The first time she'd seen him do the splits, she'd been half tempted to run over to him to see if he'd hurt himself. But he'd spun onto his back, and before she could blink, he'd flipped himself back to his feet. From there it had been more jumps, more flips, and a coordinated series of kicks and punches. After that, he'd taken off for a run, and he'd still be dripping with sweat when he returned. And, oh, how her palms itched to run them over his glistening muscles. She'd known he was fit, but watching the flexing and tensing of muscles she didn't know a man could even have turned her into a ball of overactive hormones. It should be illegal for a man to look like that.

This morning he was a little late getting up; normally by this time of day his routine would have been completed. Normally she sat in the shadows where he couldn't see her. But today the sun was up, bronzing his already tan skin, shining on his black, sweat-dampened hair. His hair was up in a simple ponytail. It should have looked feminine, would have on almost any other man, but on him, it only enhanced all that was male about him. And all she could do was openly stare.

"Can I do that, too?" Fan was on her feet, dressed in a lightweight blouse and pink shorts.

Emma nodded to the girl, and she took off like a shot on her bare feet. Anytime Bo was outside, he let the little girl sit outside with him. He didn't seem to mind her endless questions. Emma was always amused by the young girl when she would come back home with tales of China and the land she had been born in that Bo had told her about. Emma knew how important it was to Maryanne that Fan know something of where she came from. Emma had been trying to help with Fan's studies, but Mandarin was beyond her. Emma had gotten internet access back now that Bo was paying rent, and Emma had opted to let the internet teach Fan her native language. When Emma had realized that Bo was helping Fan with her words, she had cried a little at how sweet he was.

Emma had been so relieved when Bo had taken lease of

her cabin. But now that he'd been here two weeks, she found herself sometimes wishing he hadn't. He was the perfect tenant; nothing he said or did could be construed as anything but polite and courteous. The problem was with her. Watching him, feeling desire curling in her belly, made her want something she couldn't have. And Emma couldn't say it was just desire for his body; he made her desire all the things she had lost at nineteen. Her boyfriend had left to go to college, leaving her behind to wait for him. He met a woman, and the lure of her was greater than the lure of what he'd left back home. She had thought to marry him and start a family. Instead, he married his new girlfriend, and they started a family.

Emma grabbed another handful of peas and kept shelling them. Watching Bo with Fan didn't help either. Having Fan with her made her wish all the more for a daughter of her own. Seeing Bo talk to and nurture the child had Emma weaving fantasies of what it would be like if Bo were her husband and Fan her daughter. Emma knew that when Fan left, it was going to be so lonely around here. But when Emma left Bo, she had a feeling that he might leave a hole in her heart, too.

Emma took her gaze back to Bo and Fan when she heard Fan giggle. Bo was showing her a very simple pose. When Fan fell on her backside, Emma couldn't help but smile as Fan laughed even harder. Emma waved at the small girl but shook her head when Fan waved her over.

But when Bo waved her over, Emma found herself obeying. She'd spent a few quiet nights on her porch after Fan went to bed when the weather was nice. A couple of those nights Bo saw her outside when he pulled into the driveway, coming home from work. He'd come and joined her in the dark, the stars from overhead lighting his path. They'd simply chatted about his day or her day. The conversations were those of two people tentatively exploring a potential friendship. Bo had made no moves toward her, never hinted that he might feel even a fraction of the emotions that she was feeling. Looking at his glistening chest, she felt even more foolish for entertaining such fantasies about him. He could have, and probably did have, any woman he wanted. She was a simple country girl, born and raised. He was a cop from Hong Kong. Two people couldn't be more different.

Bo watched Emma as she headed his way. He was not sure what it was about her that drew him. She was goodness and kindness wrapped in the prettiest of packages. Perhaps it was because he was not accustomed to people like her. The years living with his father and the years he spent working undercover had not given him a lot of faith in humanity. But Emma, with her soft blonde hair, pretty blue eyes, and soft voice, drew him in ways he had not been before. When he was near her, she made him believe that there was good in the world, that there were people who cared more about others than themselves. Bo knew instinctively that there was nothing Emma would not do for those she loved.

"You're very impressive. You said you were good, but I'd say you're much better than good."

Bo smiled at Emma as she stood beside Fan. "There are people much better. Fan here says I am torturing you. I thought you might like to come get a closer look instead of hiding on your porch."

Emma turned beet red. She opened her mouth, but no words came out.

Bo found himself laughing, really laughing, something he had not done in ages. "I suppose that was not very gentlemanly of me. Want to learn?"

Emma shook her head. "I don't think I could do what you were doing."

Bo reached down for the glass of water he had left nearby. "What you were seeing is the culmination of many years of training. You are a bit older than the average student, but I would be happy to show you. It is great for the body and the mind."

"I'm more than a bit older than the average student. Fan here is probably the right age."

Bo knew that Emma had just turned thirty shortly before his arrival. You could see knowledge and maturity in her eyes, but her face and body looked younger. He would have pegged her as being in her early to mid-twenties if he had not known.

Emma tugged Fan to her feet. The girl was lying on the grass. "How old were you?"

Bo swallowed the glass of water before answering her. "I was older than some. I was ten. My father did not like the school I was attending and decided to switch. The school I ended up in taught martial arts. In fact, the school had one of the best martial arts masters on staff. My father had me involved in all sorts of different sports, so I was fit. When I saw the students, I became fascinated. It was all I wanted to do. I ended up being good at it. I won some local and regional competitions. I would have entered the national contests, but my father found out and was not thrilled."

Emma was surprised. "I would think your father would have been proud of you."

"My father, like I mentioned, was American. In some ways, he hated living overseas. And in some ways, he was very racist. He had a half-Chinese son, but he did not want his son to be raised as Chinese."

Emma found herself angry on behalf of the child Bo had been. "Then perhaps he should have sent you to a different school."

Bo smiled. "That he did. When I was fourteen, he sent me to Boston. He had a sister living there at the time. He had me attend high school there. Well, he did for a year anyway. But when he found out I had started attending a martial arts school in Boston, he opted to bring me home where he could keep an eye on me. He had me homeschooled for the last two years of high school. When I turned eighteen, I chose to go to a university on the mainland. He could not exactly stop me, and he did want me to get my degree."

"I take it you still studied martial arts without his permission."

Bo nodded but did not elaborate. His father had not been happy with him, but at some point, he decided that knowing martial arts might come in handy. At twenty, Bo had become his father's bodyguard. Looking into Emma's earnest gaze, there was no way he was going to elaborate.

His father had been an evil man. Though he would not call Emma naive, he did consider her innocent.

Ping Biao's arrival in her life had been an aberration. Men like him and his father did not exist in her tidy world. Bo wanted to keep it that way. Sitting on her porch in the evenings, her curvy thigh brushing up against his, he wanted nothing more than to take a taste of her. He knew she would be sweet. But he was not sweet. And he had no business even thinking about kissing her, much less acting on his wayward thoughts.

Bo set his glass back on the grass. He took Emma's hand. "Here. First, you take your stance."

Emma, feeling self-conscious, took a wide-leg stance as he instructed. She smiled when Fan did the same.

Bo very slowly took her through a series of simple, fluid movements. Fan ended up doing a somersault and then giggled while lying on the grass, but Emma, her eyes serious, followed his every move. She had an innate grace in her movements.

Bo went back to his original stance. Then he straightened. "That was very good. You are a natural."

Emma was sweating slightly, her muscles a little sore from the unaccustomed movements. She always thought of herself as in shape because of the physical work she did with her gardening, but she was a little winded.

"You have a visitor."

Emma glanced down the road and saw a van pulling into her drive. "You have very good hearing. That's Fan's playdate."

The minivan started heading toward the house but

stopped at the cabin when the driver noticed Emma. Emma was pretty sure it was Bo she was looking at.

"I should go take a shower." Bo tugged Fan back to her feet, gave Emma a slight bow, and headed inside.

Irene Collins rolled down the window. "Have mercy, who was that?"

Fan twirled. "That's Bo. He's nice."

Emma walked toward the van. "That was Bo Lee. He's the new police officer in town. He's renting the cabin."

"My Kenny can only dream of having muscles like that. You two getting cozy?"

Emma shook her head. "Drive on up to the house and we can chat over coffee. I'm sure Kenny Jr. would like to get out of his car seat."

Fan took Emma's hand as they made their way back to the house. Irene met them at the door. Emma grabbed the peas from the porch as she watched Fan take off to her toy box. Kenny Jr. followed. "Come on into the kitchen."

"Seriously, you two looked cozy. Not that that would be a bad thing, you know. You could use some male companionship." Irene took the cup of coffee Emma had brewed earlier.

"So you always say. But like Fan said, he's nice. He's also been here a couple of weeks now, so we've gotten to know him."

"And why was he outside half-naked and sweaty?"

Emma blushed. "He was exercising."

"And you were just, what, joining in? I heard rumors about a Chinese cop. Seems sort of odd, given that we're in the heartland and all. He's been the talk of the town. Of course, there is the usual assortment of people not too happy to see a foreigner living in their midst."

"That's on them. He doesn't strike me as the type to worry about it much. But there have been a few people not happy to see Fan. Ticks me off."

"Old community, small community, and some small minds. I think if you like him, you should take advantage of the situation. It's not like there are a lot of single men. I assume he's single."

"Yes. But we're worlds apart. Literally and figuratively. He was born in Hong Kong. I figure he'll eventually get bored and go back home. I got the impression he hasn't been in the U.S. long, and I get the feeling he's not very happy here. I think it's the food."

Irene finished her coffee. "I've eaten Chinese food at that place two towns over. It was good. Maybe you should take him out on a date. I can watch Fan. Maybe keep her overnight."

Emma blushed again. "I doubt he's interested, but should I need you to watch Fan, I'll let you know."

Irene patted her hand. "Lonnie was a long time ago. He's married with four kids. It's time you got over him. A scorching affair with a hottie like that guy over there would get you over him really fast."

Emma hated it when people threw Lonnie in her face. Everyone assumed Emma was still pining for him, including Lonnie and Lonnie's wife, Allison. Any time Emma ran into Allison in town, it was always awkward. If there was an audience, Allison would give her a smug smile, flaunt her children, then go back about her business. If there wasn't an audience, Emma saw the insecure side of Allison, the side that always wondered if her husband would stray if Emma made herself available. Emma didn't know how to go about assuring the woman that she wasn't still pining for Lonnie. But Emma figured there wasn't much she could say or do to ease the woman's fears. And to be honest, she wasn't inclined to do so.

Irene pushed the cup back. "I should get going. Is Fan all set to go? I have my extra car seat already in the van. Becca is waiting for us."

Emma grabbed Fan's backpack. It had a change of clothes and snacks. Usually, she and Irene met up at Becca's place with the kids once a week, but Emma needed to get some work done in her greenhouse. She had been gathering seeds and planting new clippings. The garden store in town was going to buy out her inventory when she moved, and the more inventory she had, the more money she would get.

"I appreciate you taking Fan for the day. She loves playing in the greenhouse, but I don't get much work done."

"No problem. We'll be back after dinner."

Emma gave Fan a kiss as she buckled her into the car seat and stashed her bag on the floor. The kids waved as Irene pulled out of the driveway. Sighing, and feeling sad, Emma headed to the greenhouse.

Of all that she had, the land, the house, the fields, it was her greenhouse she was going to miss the most. It used to be that when she walked through the glass doors, a sense of peace and happiness overcame her. This was hers. This was what she always wanted. But now, as it had been since the bank had sent her the final notice of foreclosure, walking through the doors was bittersweet. Just like the house and the cabin, the new owners wouldn't have much use for her greenhouse. It was possible they would rent the house out, and Bo had a lease for at least a year if he wanted it, but she didn't imagine the next owner or tenants would get use out of her greenhouse, or if they did, they wouldn't treasure it the way she did.

Taking a deep breath, she got to work. Her flowers were her favorites, though she grew a variety of ivies and grasses as well. She went and held a bright pink bloom in her fingers.

A man's voice broke the silence of the room. "A China rose."

Emma's hand dropped, and she turned to see Bo standing in the doorway. She noticed how quick he was to close the door behind him so as not to let out the warm, moist air.

"Yes. You have a good eye. In America, we call them hibiscus."

Bo came and touched the bloom Emma had just released. "More like familiarity. My father's home had many of these flowers planted around the house. They were fragrant, and their bright pink color was a contrast to the starkness of his home. I could smell the blooms in my bedroom when the wind was just right."

Emma stood still next to him; her eyes fixed on his fingers as they lightly stroked the petals. There was such softness and sensitivity in those strong hands. "Sounds like a happy memory."

Bo nodded, thinking it was only one of a small handful

of happy memories he had in a lifetime of bad ones. But those bright, blooming flowers were one. "You said I should stop in if I wanted to see what was in here."

Despite needing to get to work, she wasn't about to turn him away. "Yes. And I meant it. I have the China roses, and I have some other roses. I have climbing roses, shrub roses, and tea roses. Over here I have carnations, hydrangeas, and lilies."

Bo followed Emma while she walked him through her plants. She had some hardy grasses, some fruit trees that were still seedlings, and a host of ivies. She had plants he had never heard of, and some pretty exotic ones. He stopped in the middle of the greenhouse and just breathed in the fragrant air. "You have created a small paradise under this roof, Emma. You amaze me."

Emma blushed at the compliment. His words echoed how she felt about her small oasis in the middle of Texas. "I've always wanted to visit someplace tropical. To see and smell all the life that is there. But this is almost as good. I love every moment I spend here. I spend most of my days in here, absorbing the life around me."

"I can see why. Can I help?"

Emma stopped in her tracks. She had been heading toward a different row of plants to show him. "Don't you need to go to work?"

Bo pushed up the sleeves of his white shirt, revealing sinewy muscles. "I am off today. And I cannot think of a better place to spend it, if you do not mind an amateur in your midst."

Emma gave him a smile and shook her head. "I don't

mind at all. I was going to do some repotting today. And I was going to cull some plants and prep them for sale. Fan is going to spend the day with friends so I can get some work done."

Bo glanced over to where Emma's gaze had fallen. On a small bench were toddler-sized gardening tools in bright pink plastic. He picked up a small plastic trowel. "I think I can handle it."

Emma laughed at his joke, surprised and pleased that he had made one, and her mood lightened. "If you don't mind, I could use the help. I used to have a high school student helping me, but I couldn't afford to pay her anymore and had to let her go."

Bo declined the pair of gardening gloves Emma offered him and joined her at a workbench. Within twenty minutes, he had dirt up to his elbows, and his white t-shirt was streaked with it. He listened carefully as Emma told him what to do and followed her movements exactly.

"You've got a nice touch with the plants. You never want to manhandle them. You want to touch them gently."

Bo nodded. "Like a man should a woman."

Emma choked on her words, but Bo didn't seem to notice what he'd said. Emma's thoughts strayed to those hands on her skin, touching her as gently as he did her plants. She couldn't help but stare helplessly at him.

Bo glanced up to see Emma staring at him. Her cheeks were flushed, and her lips slightly parted. He had seen hints of desire in her eyes before. His heart reacted to those looks, but he kept his body under ruthless control. "Emma?"

"What?" She blinked up at him.

"No."

She didn't understand. "No what?"

He touched a knuckle to her flushed cheek. "Just no."

She immediately flushed again and took a step back. Embarrassed that he obviously knew what she was thinking and wasn't thinking the same, she turned away from him.

Bo cursed silently at her sudden retreat. He had not meant to hurt her feelings. "Emma."

Emma shook her head. "No, I'm sorry. You're right. It's just that I like you, and I forget sometimes."

This time it was he who did not understand. "Forget what?"

"Nothing. I'm sorry, though, all the same. I didn't mean to make it awkward. I can finish this up myself."

"I will finish helping. This is very soothing. Good for the soul."

Because he seemed sincere, and she couldn't exactly throw him out, she came back to where he was. She finished showing him what she wanted done, keeping her eyes down and off of him. Then she went to the other workbench and got started on her own. She had some seeds she wanted to plant and cultivate. Starter plants were always big sellers, as most people didn't want to start from the beginning but wanted to plant something and see immediate results.

Over the course of the next few hours, Bo took directions and worked alongside Emma. He was sorry he had made her uncomfortable around him. But he did not want her getting any ideas about him. He was not the man for her, not even temporarily. It had been a very long time since he had touched a woman, since he had lost himself in the warmth of one. And if ever there was a woman made to tempt a man like him, it was Emma. She was petite and curvy in all the right places. Her mouth was as pink and as lush as the China roses he had admired. She was intelligent and hard-working. She adored Fan, taking her adopted niece into her heart and into her home. For a man like Bo, who had never had a family as most people knew them, Emma was a temptation like he had never known.

Emma stretched her back and took a look around the greenhouse, her eyes no longer focused on her plants. With Bo's help, she had accomplished so much more than she had expected to. Forgetting her earlier embarrassment, she smiled at him. "I can't thank you enough for helping me. I just need to give everything a nice soak, and I'll be done for the day."

Bo wiped the sweat from his brow and looked around. "I see why you enjoy this so much. There is a sense of accomplishment."

Emma pulled the sprayer that was mounted above her plants. "Perhaps there is a bit of a farmer inside you."

"What time is Fan coming home?"

Emma looked up at the clock she had hidden behind some plants. "Not for a few hours. Irene is staying for dinner, so Fan won't be back until probably seven or eight. When I go, I don't get home until about then."

Bo looked up to where Emma was looking. It was only a little after four. "Let me treat you to dinner."

Emma was startled by the invitation. "That hardly

seems fair when I had you working all day. I owe you dinner."

Bo glanced at his dirty hands. "No, I think I owe you. Let me go wash up, and I will meet you in thirty."

Emma wasn't given a chance to argue. In fact, she hadn't even agreed to go. But Bo strode away, his long legs carrying him out the door before she could protest again. She finished soaking her plants, then went inside to wash up. She tied up her hair and showered quickly. She was grateful he said thirty minutes. It left her no time to fuss with her clothes. She pulled on a pair of jeans and a blouse before heading to the bathroom to fluff out her hair and dust some powder on her face.

She was coming down the stairs when she heard him knock on her door. She had left the door open, and the screen wasn't latched. He didn't notice her at first, so she took a moment to take him in. His hair was pulled back in a low ponytail again, and he was wearing a pair of jeans this time and another chest-hugging t-shirt, this one in black. She stopped breathing for a moment when his eyes found hers.

"Ready?"

Emma nodded and hurried down the stairs. "We'll have to eat local. I want to be back by seven."

"Is there someplace else to eat, not at that diner where I met you?"

"There is a place. It's nicer than the diner, but I don't know if you'll find anything to your liking."

Bo shrugged. "I will risk it."

Chapter Four

Emma was mostly quiet during the drive, except for when she gave him directions. Bo still was not sure what possessed him to ask her to dinner. He was sorry that he had embarrassed her earlier today, but it was not difficult to know what a woman was thinking when she looked at a man like that. He knew the best way to discourage her was to be honest and tell her upfront he was not interested. The problem was that he was interested. But he had no business thinking the lustful thoughts he had been having about Emma.

He would like to chalk it up to the fact that she was different from the women he was used to. Of course, what he mostly chalked it up to was the fact that he had not been with a woman in what seemed like ages. But one thing he did know was that if he were to end his celibacy, it should not be with a woman like her.

Bo liked to think he understood people and what motivated them. He also liked to think he was a good judge of character. Being around Emma the past few weeks and digging further into her background, just to be sure he was right about her, he knew he could take Emma at face value. She was a single woman who was mostly alone in the world. Her cousin was not going to be much help when she resurfaced. Bo had been digging and was pretty sure that as soon as Maryanne Biao showed up, she would take Fan with her into hiding and do her best to never be found. But Bo was worried about what Biao might do when Maryanne did resurface. Jonas had the best people in the FBI trying to find him and had yet to do so. Neither Jonas nor Bo understood why Biao had attacked his wife and then disappeared again. Coming out of hiding, even for that brief time, was not wise.

Bo kept telling himself that he was just here to make sure Fan was okay and in good hands, but the more time he spent around Emma, the more concerned he became for her well-being. And though Bo swore he did not want to be involved in the hunt for Biao, should he show up, he would have no compunction about taking him out.

"You turn here, and then it's on the left about a mile." Emma tried not to stare, but she couldn't help it. She didn't know what was on his mind, but he looked a bit fierce.

Bo pulled into the restaurant and came to help Emma from the SUV. He took her hand as he led her to the building. He could not help but notice that Emma seemed surprised by his touch.

A rather robust-looking hostess took them to a table. He took the menu and thanked the woman.

"You do have quite the effect on women, Bo." Emma smiled at him. Though the hostess left their table, the woman kept looking back at them.

"Is that a good thing or a bad thing?" Bo set the menu down and focused on Emma.

Emma shrugged. "I suppose that would depend. Good

for you, but probably not so good for the trail of broken hearts you leave in your wake."

Bo realized she was teasing him. He smiled and opened his menu. "I will try not to break any hearts tonight."

Emma giggled and opened her menu. "I hope you find something to your liking. My friend Irene was telling me there is a Chinese restaurant a couple of towns over. I don't know if it's authentic or not, but you may want to check it out."

"If my order ever arrives, I will not have to drive there to get authentic. I still owe you a meal."

Emma waved at the open menu. "I'd say you more than fulfilled that promise."

Bo shook his head. "No. I promised you authentic Chinese food. Not just a meal."

Emma wasn't going to turn down the offer should he make it in the future. "Then I'll look forward to it. I like the noodles."

Bo hid his grin behind his menu. Deciding, though probably not fresh, he would get the fish. The one nice thing about having stayed in both Los Angeles and Virginia was that he could get fresh seafood. Not interested in tepid tea or soda, he opted for a glass of water.

Emma ordered a pasta dish and a glass of iced tea. "I'm not much of a drinker. Are you?"

Bo was surprised by the question. "Not much. I will share a beer with my brother or share a glass of wine with my sister-in-law, but like most things here in the U.S., I prefer the alcoholic beverages from back home."

"Something tells me that you might not make it as a

permanent citizen."

Bo shrugged. "Not everything in China is all great either. I have no doubt I will discover things I like given time. Like pizza. I do like to order pizza. I think it was all I ate when I went to school in Boston."

Emma couldn't help but laugh. She couldn't actually see him eating it. Emma stopped laughing when she saw who was being seated a few tables over.

Bo glanced to where Emma was looking. A couple, probably around Emma's age, took a seat. The tall blonde woman was trying not to glare but was failing.

Bo did not say anything at first. When he did finally speak, they simply chatted about inconsequential things. When their food was delivered, they focused on sampling their meals. His fish was not bad, and the veggies were not soggy, which pleased him.

Halfway through, he could no longer pretend not to notice the blonde. "Who is she? She looks like she would like to see you drop through the floor and disappear."

Emma didn't bother to pretend she didn't know what he was talking about. "That is Allison. She thinks I am going to steal her husband away."

Bo's eyes narrowed as he took a closer look at the man at the table. He was maybe five-nine, a little stocky. He had sandy brown hair and a beard that covered most of his face. Not impressed with what he saw, he turned back to Emma. "Why?"

Emma took a bite of her pasta, doing her best to ignore Allison. She knew the woman was still glaring at her from time to time. "Probably because she stole him from me."

Bo watched her face but could not tell what she was thinking. She did not seem overly worried about the other woman, but what about the man? Bo felt a wave of possessiveness come over him and tried to tamp it down.

Emma set her fork down, unable to eat with Bo's complete focus on her. "His name is Lonnie. And no, I am not trying to take him from her. Not that she would ever believe that. They have four daughters, and even if I still held a torch for him, which I don't, I wouldn't try to separate a man from his children."

"She does not believe that."

It wasn't a question, but she answered it anyway. "No. When she's in public, she glares. When no one is around, she goes the opposite direction. And if her children are near, she gears herself up to do battle. It's tiring, really, but she won't believe I don't want her husband. Neither do most of the people in town. Poor little Emma, still pining away for her lost love."

Bo could not stop his smile. "I take it you are not pining for him."

"Believe it or not, I have had boyfriends since him. I can't say he didn't hurt me, because he did. Deeply at the time. But time heals wounds."

"But you have not married."

"No, and neither have you. That does not mean you are pining over a woman."

Bo supposed that was true. But some wounds went very deep, and though scarred, were not necessarily healed. "Perhaps being seen with me will make people believe you are no longer pining for him."

Emma had to bite her tongue at her immediate reaction to his words. She thought that if he kissed her, people might believe that, but Bo had already made his feelings clear. She was not willing to throw herself at an unwilling man. Instead, she nodded. "Perhaps. There will be talk since it's widely known you are living on my property. Some will think the worst."

"Gossip is the same around the world. Rarely is there much truth in it, but that never stops people from talking."

"There are other people here who are staring at you. Does it bother you?"

Bo knew what she was talking about. In places like Los Angeles, no one paid him any notice. But since arriving in rural Texas, he had been the subject of a lot of stares. "No, it does not bother me. Most people are staring out of curiosity. Curiosity is not a bad thing. Others will stare for more sinister reasons, but I do not pay them any mind."

Emma finished her tea and pushed her plate back. "It's a good attitude to have. So you know my dark secret. Any women hanging around that might come calling?"

Bo finished his meal as well and signaled for their waitress. "No, there are no women who will come calling. You are the first woman in some time I have gone out with."

"Yes, but we're just friends. Most men usually crave female companionship of a more romantic type from time to time."

Bo was a bit amused by her candid words and flushed cheeks. "I like sex if that is your question. And I like women if that is your other question."

Emma was glad she had finished her drink; she might

have choked on it. "I wasn't hinting that you might be abnormal or anything."

They were interrupted by the waitress. Bo paid for their meal, left a generous tip, and led Emma to his vehicle. Bo opened the door for her and gently closed it when she was seated.

Emma wished she had kept her mouth shut. Bo didn't seem offended by her question, but it just surprised her. The men she knew, including Lonnie back before he had married, would have jumped at the opportunity she had presented to him earlier today. As far as she had experienced, which admittedly wasn't a lot, men didn't say no.

The ride back was quieter than the ride in. Bo didn't seem to need her help navigating his way back home. As soon as they pulled into the driveway, Irene pulled up behind them.

Bo opened Emma's door and helped her out once again. "I should let you get Fan settled. Thank you for coming to dinner with me. It is good to have a friend."

Though it made her heart ache a bit that friendship was all he wanted from her, she still was happy he wanted that much. He was a nice man, one who could talk about almost anything. And though their meal tonight had centered on topics she would just as soon not talk about, it had still been nice. Her heart fluttered when he gave her a slight bow and got back into his SUV to park it at his cottage.

She sighed and helped Fan out of her car seat.

"I see you took my advice." Irene grinned at her through the open window.

"It was just dinner. Sorry, no juicy tidbits to share."

"Oh, well. Maybe next time. My offer is open."

Emma held Fan in her arms until Irene drove away. She then carried the sleepy child inside. After settling Fan in bed and reading her a bedtime story, she took herself to bed early. Tomorrow would be another early day. And if she were lucky, Bo would be outside again in the morning, where she could admire him from the shadows of her porch once again.

* * *

Bo checked his email when he got back inside the cottage. He needed a distraction to keep his mind off of Emma. He frowned when he saw a message from his brother Jonas to call him. Jonas was one of the few people who had his phone number, but more often than not, Jonas would request that he call him instead. Bo picked up the cell phone he stashed in the nightstand and dialed his brother.

"Hello, Brother."

"I see you got my message." Jonas settled back into bed beside his wife.

"I hope I am not calling at a bad time."

Jonas glanced at his wife, who was smiling at him from beneath the sheets. "Not yet. But I know better. You would not feel bad if you had called at a bad time."

Bo liked his brother, though he had only known him for less than a year. He also liked his sister-in-law, Lian. Lian had grown up in China, so he had a lot in common with her. On the rare occasions he saw her, they would talk about the different places they had both been to. Lian was in the process of planning a month-long trip back home so she could show Jonas. The pair was looking forward to the time off, especially Lian, who had never thought to make the U.S. her permanent home until she met Jonas. But until Biao was caught, Bo imagined the trip would have to wait.

"I do assume you had a reason for emailing me?" Bo stripped off his clothes and grabbed a pair of comfortable pants. He found jeans restrictive but wore them in public to help blend in. Not that the jeans really helped him do that, he mused.

"Maryanne Biao surfaced."

Bo was not at all surprised. Emma was expecting the woman to make an appearance any day now. "But no Biao?"

"No. We've got agents nearby in case she does show up at her cousin's home. We want to be prepared should Biao come looking for her again."

Bo was not convinced Biao would bother. "Like I told the sheriff here, Biao would not be overly concerned about a wife and daughter. If he had a son, then it would be different."

Jonas had heard Bo's theory before but wasn't sure he bought into it. "And like I said before, he tracked her down when she was in Virginia, knowing full well the FBI was hunting him. He also showed up at Emma McKinnon's home, and we didn't think he would. If Miss McKinnon hadn't run him off, he might very well have killed his wife and daughter."

"I will make you one promise, Jonas. Should Biao show

up here, I can guarantee he will get nowhere near Maryanne, Fan, or Emma."

Jonas was quiet for a moment. He spoke softly when he finally broke the silence. "What is she like? She must be something special if she has gotten your attention."

Bo scowled at the phone. "I did not say she was special."

"Let's just say I know that tone. I'm still not sure why you're out there. You say you are not hunting Biao, but you followed his daughter."

Bo had not told Jonas the truth about Fan. He was still waiting on the DNA results, though he knew what they would say. But Jonas would require proof, and Bo would have it before he told him. "I am the cautious type. Fan is just a child. I want to be sure she is safe."

"I might believe that if you weren't such a hard man. What is one child to you?"

Bo knew that Jonas had done some extensive research on him once he had access to the right files. When Bo first met Jonas, Jonas believed him to be a triad leader. Then Bo had to come clean and told him he was an undercover cop from Hong Kong. Between them, they had shut down a very large human trafficking and gun trafficking ring. Biao might still be alive, but his dreams of taking Bo down and becoming a triad leader were dead.

"Are you there?"

Bo shook himself back into the present. "I care. That is all I am willing to say on the subject right now. You will get the rest of your answers later."

Jonas knew not to push. "Just remember you are not

there in an official capacity. If you interfere, I will have to arrest you."

Bo knew his brother meant every word. "I am official. I took a job as a police officer here. All legal."

That threw Jonas. "You're working as a cop?"

"Small town. I did not need so many fancy qualifications. I more than qualify, do I not?"

"Fine. I suppose that should make me happy. When are you coming home? You can't avoid Naiwen forever."

Actually, he could. In fact, it was terribly easy, but he did not want to fight with his brother over it. "Your mother does not want to see me."

Jonas jumped into the argument he always gave him. "She is our mother, not just mine. You should give her a chance to get to know you."

"She knows all that is important."

Jonas would have argued further but stopped when Lian's soft voice came over the line and calmed him. "You did what you had to do, though it wasn't pretty. Maybe one day you can forgive yourself."

Bo was taken aback. That was a new argument. He would have argued, but there was truth in Lian's words. His own words were soft when he spoke. "For some, there is no forgiveness, nor is it deserved. I will let you know when Maryanne shows. Emma is waiting for her return. They will be safe, though again I do not believe Biao will show."

The two men spoke for a few moments longer before Bo hung up. He went to the window that faced Emma's home. The lights were off, except for the porch light Emma kept on at night. He imagined Emma had put Fan to bed before heading to her own room. He imagined she had changed into some prim nightgown before climbing into bed. His body ached because he wished he could climb into that bed with her.

Bo turned away. Once upon a time, he would have taken Emma up on her offer. It would have been much easier to get close to Fan if he started a physical relationship with Emma. Many women tended to be too trusting of the men they slept with. There had been one too many women who had trusted him and should not have.

Bo lay down on the small bed, having not yet replaced it. Men could be too trusting of the women they slept with, too. Bo did not think about Chingmy often anymore. He had loved her, trusted her, and while she shared his bed, she was betraying him. He supposed he did not blame her. A woman in her position had to look out for herself. But Bo would have given her anything, done anything to protect her. She had not trusted him, nor had she loved him. And in the end, he could not protect her from his father.

Bo remained restless throughout the night, sleeping little. It was four a.m. when he heard his computer ping. Climbing from the bed, he opened his computer. He thought it might be his brother again, but it was his friend from Hong Kong who was running the DNA sample for him. He opened the report and smiled with satisfaction. He was right. Fan was his sister.

Bo saved the report and locked his laptop. He went to the kitchen and pulled out a canister of tea. He set a kettle of water to boil and looked back out the window at the main house while he contemplated his next move.

Bo knew that Biao did not realize the child he called his own was not his. His father had hired Gua, Fan's mother, to get close to Biao. Biao had taken to her, or rather had taken her, and when she turned up pregnant, his father had told Biao that he should keep her. Bo had not known back then. His father had many women, including his own mother, whom he kept under lock and key. It was not until Howard was dead and Bo had gone through his father's personal papers that he realized Biao's daughter, Fan, was really Howard's. Fan had the look of her mother, so it was not obvious that her father was not Chinese.

Bo poured the water over his tea and let it steep as he thought about that day. Bo would not be surprised if Howard had fathered dozens of children. Before his father's death, Bo had only known of one brother, but his brother was older than he was and could take care of himself. Finding out his brother was an FBI agent had also given him peace of mind. But as he looked down at the picture of Fan, he could not write her off as just another one of Howard's unwanted children. Her sweet face had haunted him.

Bo took his tea outside. The night air was chilly, but he needed it to clear his head. He knew he would have to tell Jonas eventually. Jonas would do what he could to protect the child who was his half-sister. Jonas was dedicated to not only his job but his family. Jonas had been adopted in his teens, years after his mother Naiwen had sent him to America to get away from his father, who would have molded him into his image. Bo was the second child of Howard and Naiwen, and he had been kept from her, spending his early years being meticulously groomed to take over Howard's business one day. And Howard had been successful until Bo was in his late teens.

Bo sipped his tea, his gaze on the house where Fan slept peacefully. Bo knew it was a waste of time to dwell on the past. He could not change it. All he could do was move forward, do what he could to atone for the past, and make sure that Fan had the childhood that had been denied to both him and Jonas.

Chapter Five

Emma breathed deeply as she stood beside Bo, following the fluid movements of his body but with much less grace.

Bo placed a hand on Emma's spine to keep her body in the proper form. "Any day now, you will be better than I am."

Emma snorted unladylike at that. In the past week since their dinner, Bo had come to the house to fetch her to exercise with him in the morning before he left for work. Her body, still not used to the movements he was teaching her, was sore. The stretching felt great, and she was convinced she had more energy, but her muscles still trembled toward the end. Bo would hardly have worked up a sweat yet. For him, that would come later when he put his body through more rigorous exercise. She would sit in the grass, admiring his skill as much as his body.

She had been surprised to find him knocking on her door early in the morning after their dinner to invite her to join him. She had still been wrapped up in a long terry cloth robe to ward off the early morning chill, sipping her first cup of coffee. Fan had been sleeping and would be for a couple more hours yet. Bo had looked intense that morning, something about him different from how he'd been the night before. But because her heart raced whenever he was near, she had nodded, ran up the stairs, and pulled on the first thing she thought might be appropriate for the workout he had in mind. The baggy sweats and t-shirt were stained with dirt from her greenhouse, as were many of her clothes.

"I could do this for another twenty years and not be as good as you." Emma stumbled a bit, but Bo's hand kept her in place.

"In twenty years, I will have slowed down."

Emma breathed deeply and let it out slowly like he'd shown her. "Yeah, but I'll be twenty years older, too. We're not that far apart in age."

Bo shifted so he could guide Emma into the next pose. "I forget you are not as young as you look."

Emma glanced up at him, partially amused, partially annoyed, and a whole lot aware of his hands on her body. "I think that might have been a compliment, but I can't be sure."

Bo's mouth came near her ear. "Definitely a compliment."

Emma shivered in his grasp as she felt his breath on her neck. Unable to help herself, she looked over her shoulder until she could see his face.

Bo's gaze dropped to Emma's soft mouth, and his hands tightened on her hips. It had seemed like a nice, friendly gesture to invite Emma to work out with him in the mornings. Both of them were morning people, and he genuinely enjoyed her company. Sometimes she made him laugh, something he had not done a lot in his life, and sometimes she made him think and expand how he saw the world. He was never bored with her, never eager to move on to something else. She was calming and soothing in a world filled with so much chaos.

But times like this, when she looked at him with desire filling her eyes, he wished he had never come here. He liked to think he was a man with great self-control. And in most things, he was. But holding Emma close, feeling the warmth of her body pressed against his, made him forget that he should not touch, that he should not crave her with every part of his being.

"Bo?" Emma turned a bit so she could get closer to him.

Bo's hands tightened further, his mouth only a few inches from hers. He could practically taste her. When Emma's eyes closed, willing to put herself in his care, it took everything in him not to kiss her.

Emma's eyes opened when he released her. She stumbled toward him but caught herself before she took a full step. Feeling hurt but not wanting him to know, she turned away from him and tried to focus on the routine he had taught her.

Bo took a step back. "Emma?"

Emma's chin dropped to her chest. She didn't want to hear it. "Please don't say it. I should probably go. I have work to do today, and Maryanne is due to arrive tonight."

The mention of Maryanne's name had him swallowing what he was going to say. He knew he should explain to Emma that he liked her but was not the man for her. Instead, he dropped what he was going to say in favor of focusing on what she had just said. "You had not mentioned she was coming so soon. Fan must be ecstatic."

Emma picked her hoodie up from the ground and tucked it under her arm. "She called late last night. She didn't want to show up unexpectedly. Fan doesn't know. Just in case Maryanne runs late, I didn't want to get her hopes up. Plus, I never would have gotten Fan to bed if she knew her mother was due to arrive."

Bo kept his voice flat when he spoke. "You never did say why Maryanne was away."

Emma was cautious as she replied. She hadn't thought about it, but it was more than possible Martin had told Bo what happened last spring. And given that he was living on her property, she would be more surprised if Martin had not mentioned it. "No, I didn't. What have you heard?"

Bo figured the truth would be in his favor. "Sheriff Townsend said that she has an abusive husband. That he showed up here and beat her severely. He also said that you protected her and her daughter with a shotgun you keep stashed in a closet."

Shivering now as her sweat chilled on her skin, Emma pulled her hoodie on. "It's like he said. Her husband is a dangerous man. I didn't know how much until last spring. Maryanne had to go into a rehab facility because of the extent of her injuries. She did so under a false identity so her husband couldn't find her."

"He has not been around, has he? Has he made any threats against you or Fan?" Bo took a step closer, his eyes on her face to see if he could detect any hint of a lie on her part.

"No. He made all kinds of ugly threats before he left,

but he hasn't been back. Sheriff Townsend used to come by the house once a week or so and ask me the same question. But he disappeared. I haven't heard from him since. And I know Maryanne has not."

"Why did he come?" Bo took Emma's hand and started walking her back to her house.

"Money. He thought Maryanne had taken some money from him. It's not here, and she didn't have it. She doesn't know where it went."

Bo followed Emma into her home. "How much money?"

Emma stopped in her tracks. "You sound like a cop."

Bo gently reminded her. "I am a cop. And with Maryanne coming back, it is conceivable that her husband might show up if he thinks she has his money."

"Maryanne didn't have it. He tossed her car and her bedroom when he was here. That was before he hurt her. Maryanne wouldn't have taken something like that, not if she knew he would come after her to get it back. Her only concern was protecting Fan."

Bo let Emma go upstairs. He contemplated what she said. Maryanne could very well have stolen money from Biao. It was not as if she worked and had an income of her own. Maryanne had gone off the grid after Biao's attack, and that meant she had to have some cash stashed away to stay in hiding for as long as she had. Bo would alert Jonas before he left for work, but unless Biao was tracking Maryanne, he would have no way of knowing she was on her way here. It was doubtful someone was watching Emma. This was a small town, and any stranger would stand out. He should know.

Emma came down a few minutes later to find Bo still in her home. She found him in her kitchen, instead of in the living room where she had left him. "I'm sorry, Bo. I didn't mean to be so abrupt. I've always been protective of Maryanne. She's a delicate person, in spirit and in feelings. When she got married, she was so excited and so happy. She never let on there was anything wrong. When she showed up here last spring with her adopted daughter in tow, she acted like she was just here for a visit, though I knew something was wrong. I just never guessed how bad things were for her. Her husband is a man named Ping Biao. After he left, I did some research. He's a very dangerous man. And I can only pray he never shows up here, or anywhere near Maryanne and Fan again. Once Maryanne fetches Fan, they'll leave."

Bo digested that tidbit. "Did you know Maryanne's husband before she married him?"

Emma poured them both a cup of coffee. "No. I hadn't met him at all until he came here. Maryanne had been in China studying as part of an exchange program. She met Ping while still in school. They got married and she stayed in China. A few months after their marriage, she called me and said her husband was traveling for work and that she was coming with him. She wanted to come see me. She showed up earlier than I had expected, but I didn't mind. I learned afterward from reading the news online that her husband had killed someone and that he was involved in human trafficking. It was a shock. By then, Maryanne was gone and I had Fan. I promised to take care of her, and that's what I did."

Bo came and cupped Emma's chin. "I want you to tell me if you hear from him, or if you get scared for any reason. Promise me."

Emma's knees went weak. "Am I promising the cop or the man?"

Bo backed Emma up against the counter, his body caging hers. "Does it matter?"

Emma wanted nothing more than to wrap her arms around him, but despite the nearness of his body to hers, his face wasn't friendly. "Perhaps not. But I don't know that I could deny the man if he were the one asking."

Bo pressed his advantage. "Then promise the man."

"I promise."

Bo released her, but it was with great reluctance. "I need to get ready for work. You have my cell number."

Emma nodded and watched as Bo left. Trembling, she sat at the table. She then heard footsteps on the stairs and got herself together. She had responsibilities, and it didn't do her any good to dwell on Bo and her ever-growing attraction to him.

* * *

Emma and Fan were outside playing when a taxi pulled up. It took Fan only a moment to realize who was stepping out of the car.

"Momma!" Fan ran toward her mother.

"Fan! I missed you so much." Maryanne Biao dropped to her knees so she could clutch her daughter to her, savoring the feel of her daughter in her arms again.

Emma kept back for a few moments and let mother and daughter get reacquainted. Instead, she went to the cab and pulled the luggage out. Not wanting to disturb the reunion, Emma went inside to get the money that the cab driver was owed. She paid the man and waited.

"Oh, Emma. I'm so happy to see you." Maryanne kept her daughter in her arms while she embraced her cousin.

Emma hugged her close. "You look wonderful."

"Thank you. And thank you for paying the driver. It's so good to see you."

Emma stopped and took another look at her cousin. Her delicate frame and slim figure had transformed. Her cousin was still delicate, but not slim. "And how is my future nephew doing?"

Maryanne smiled and dropped one hand to her protruding belly. "The doctor says he's fine. After I arrived at the rehab center, the doc ordered all kinds of tests. In three months or so, I expect to give birth to a healthy, very large baby boy. The doctor thinks I may need to schedule a c-section. He's not convinced I'll be able to have him naturally."

Emma carried the suitcases while Maryanne carried Fan. Emma had known Maryanne was pregnant last fall. Her cousin had admitted it when she was feeling ill and wasn't eating much. Because Emma had been concerned, her cousin had confessed. She also confessed that her husband didn't know and that she didn't want him to know. It was at that moment, the day before Biao arrived, that Emma knew for certain something wasn't right with her cousin's marriage.

"I can be there; I told you that before. Nothing is keeping me here."

Maryanne took a seat and settled Fan on her lap. The little girl buried her face in her mother's shoulder. "I am so very sorry you're losing the house. I wish I could have helped."

"It's a done deal. The paperwork has gone through, and I have until the end of the month to move out. I was hoping you could help me pack. I haven't started yet, as I didn't want it to disturb Fan."

Maryanne took her cousin's hand. "I wish you would have told me last year. My husband has more money than he knows what to do with. I could have helped."

Emma looked at Fan and held her tongue. She didn't want to confront Maryanne the moment she arrived, and she didn't want to talk about what had happened in front of Fan. "It was my problem to deal with. I'll be fine. But I could come with you."

Maryanne let Fan go when the child started squirming. She watched with tender eyes as her daughter went into the other room to get her toys so she could show her momma what Auntie Emma had gotten for her.

"The closer I get to having this baby, the more your offer appeals. But I would worry about you. You've never lived anywhere else. And I am not sure that you want to come with me where I'm going."

"You haven't said yet where you're going."

"I'm going back to China. I have friends there, friends that are not friends with Ping. And if Ping were to ever set foot back in China, he'll be killed. So I'm going back. It's the safest place for me."

Emma was completely taken aback. She hadn't realized that her cousin was going back to China. She thought she might go back to California. Maryanne had lived there for a good portion of her youth and had gone to college there until she joined the exchange program.

She was prevented from asking any more questions while Fan came back to the kitchen to tell her mother all that had happened while she was away. It wasn't until much later that evening, when Fan finally slept after her exciting day, that the two women had another chance to talk.

"I'm going to miss you." Emma tucked her legs underneath her as she settled onto the sofa.

"I'll miss you too. And so will Fan. I don't know what I would have done without you."

"You'd have figured it out. You were always the more resourceful of the two of us."

"I was the mischievous one, and you were the planner. It was rare that we got caught. And it was always thanks to you and your grand plan." Maryanne laughed while she thought of some of the trouble the two of them had gotten into together.

"You made me get out of my comfort zone. I'd say you were the adventurous one." Emma, too, was remembering the fun she and her cousin used to have. It seemed so long ago.

Maryanne started in her seat when a pair of headlights flashed past the house windows. "Who's here?"

Emma glanced out the window. "That's Bo. He's a

police officer in town, and he's been renting the cabin for the past month. Fan is a big fan, no pun intended."

Maryanne relaxed in her seat. "You didn't mention a tenant."

"He's been a blessing. The money he has been paying is going to make the down payment on an apartment in town."

"You said Fan liked him?" Maryanne yawned and stretched on the couch.

"Yes. He's Chinese."

Maryanne shot up in her seat. "What?"

"It's okay. He's a cop. I told you."

"Are you sure?" Maryanne was nervous any time she saw a Chinese face.

Emma tried to calm her cousin. "Sheriff Townsend vouched for him. I admit I had some doubts when I first heard that there was a Chinese cop in town. But I couldn't find anything about him on the internet, and the sheriff hired him. You've nothing to worry about."

Maryanne's eyes narrowed as she studied her cousin. Then she smiled at her. "You like him."

"I do. But he doesn't like me, not like that." It hurt to say it, but she didn't want her cousin getting any ideas about her and Bo.

"Then he's a fool. And you don't want a fool anyway."

Emma wished she could adopt that attitude, but she couldn't. Every day she spent with Bo, she got more and more attached. She hadn't mentioned to Bo yet that her time was running out. She wanted to be out by the end of next week before the police came to remove her from the property. Most of all, she wanted to remember her last days here with fondness. "You can meet him tomorrow. You should get some rest."

"That's probably a good idea. Pregnancy has taken its toll, and Fan wore me out."

Emma turned off the lights as she followed her cousin upstairs. "She was just so excited to see you."

Maryanne stopped outside Fan's bedroom door, where she would be sleeping on an air mattress. "You did so much more than you had to. The Chinese lessons, the toys, her own room. I can never repay you for what you did for me. I never should have come here, but I didn't know where else to turn."

"We're family. No thanks are necessary. Just promise me you'll keep in touch with me. Maybe one day I can visit you."

Maryanne hugged her cousin. "Get a passport. You're going to want to meet your cousin after he's born."

Emma held Maryanne for a moment before letting her go and heading to her own bedroom. She went to her window and saw Bo sitting outside on his small porch. Not feeling at all tired, she hurried downstairs and grabbed her coat and shoes.

"Good evening, Emma." Bo had seen her in the bedroom window and had watched as she crossed the yard to him.

"Good evening. I saw you outside."

Bo gestured to the step. "Did your cousin arrive safely?"

"Yes. She's gone to bed. Fan wore her out."

Bo chuckled. "I imagine she did. A girl needs her

mother."

"Yes." Emma turned her eyes up to the thousands of stars shining down on them.

"Such sad eyes tonight." Bo brushed a tear from Emma's cheek.

"Maryanne said she's going to go back to China. I didn't realize she was taking Fan so far away. And I should have told you sooner, but next week is my last week here. I can't even imagine what the future holds. I want this moment to last forever."

Emma wasn't sure when her tears started to fall in earnest, but knew the exact moment when Bo pulled her against him. She didn't cry long. When the tears were gone, she remained in his arms. She smiled when she felt his lips on her hair.

Bo held Emma under the stars, his mind only able to focus on the woman he held. She would be gone from his life soon. Bo would not be remaining in Texas much longer. He had confirmation that Fan was his sister. He knew Jonas would keep Maryanne on his radar now that she had come out of hiding. Jonas was sending an agent out here to tail her when she left. And if Maryanne Biao planned to hop a plane back to the Mainland, then should Jonas choose to detain her, she would be easy to find. The problem was it would be easy for Biao to find her, too, once she tried to board a plane under her real identity.

Bo had called Jonas last night and told him the full story of what had happened. Both Bo and Jonas were pretty sure that Maryanne did have the money Biao was looking for or had at least stashed it for safekeeping. That could put both Fan and Emma in danger. No longer feeling confident that Biao would not show up, Bo planned to keep a close eye on Emma.

Emma sighed and pulled away from Bo. "I wish things were different. Thanks for letting me cry on you."

Bo brushed the hair back from her face. "You might be the first."

"No previous girlfriends weeping on your shoulder?"

Bo's thumb brushed Emma's mouth. "Not that I can recall. Though when I am here with you like this, it is hard to remember that there have ever been other women."

Stunned by his words, Emma stared at Bo.

Bo got to his feet and pulled Emma up beside him, his arms coming around her. "Maybe it is the stars. Or maybe it is the moon. Or maybe it is because I am a weak man. Or maybe it is just you. I need you, Emma."

Chapter Six

Emma was sure that no man had ever said anything sweeter to her. Nerves threatened to take hold while Bo looked down at her, asking her for an answer to his unspoken question. "I thought you didn't like me that way."

Bo brushed a kiss on her temple, then her cheek. "How could I not?"

"Then why?" She shivered, but it wasn't from the cold.

"I cannot explain it. But I am not the man for you Emma. You deserve better."

"Better than you?" Emma wrapped her arms around Bo's neck. She tipped her head to give him access to her neck.

"Yes." His teeth grazed the soft, exposed skin.

"There is no one else, Bo. There hasn't been for so long."

Bo pulled back. Her eyes were partially closed while she clung to him. Knowing it was wrong, knowing he should keep his hands off her, but unable to make himself obey, he unzipped her jacket. Wrapping his arms around her waist, he lifted her. He pulled away only long enough to open his cabin door and close it behind them.

"You will leave, and so will I. Be sure, Emma. It cannot be undone."

She would leave the farm. One day he would leave Texas. But maybe, when he did, she could go with him. But whether she went with him or never saw him again, her answer remained the same. She shrugged out of her jacket. "No regrets. Never."

Groaning and abandoning himself to fate, he kissed Emma for the first time. Her mouth softened under his as she raised herself on her toes to meet him. Not breaking their kiss, he picked her up and set her on the narrow bed. He then pulled away to gaze down at her as he leaned over her.

Emma heard the words he spoke, though they didn't make sense to her. But the look in his eyes told her that his words were of need and desire, and it was enough for her.

Bo took his time kissing her and learning the taste of her, reveling in the small sounds she made. This might be the only night they were together like this, and he wanted to memorize every moment. Her t-shirt was disposed of, and he tasted every bit of her. Her arms and shoulders were toned from the physical work she did. Her belly was flat, and he could not help but caress the soft skin there. But her breasts were now what held his attention. He tugged the bra straps from her shoulders, kissing her from her collar bone to the tops of her breasts. She wore a simple, functional bra, and he stripped it from her. She arched herself to him, her eyes open on his.

Bo's touch was slow and arousing. He did not rush but savored. She wanted to unbutton his uniform shirt, but his hands stopped hers. He pinned them softly to the mattress while his mouth bit and suckled her breasts. Heat pooled in her lower body, and her legs parted to cradle him closer.

Bo sat back and stripped off his shirt. He tossed it on top of where he had tossed Emma's.

"Every day when you are outside, stripped to the waist, my hands itch to touch."

Bo leaned down to kiss her again. "I could feel your eyes on me. I wanted your touch."

Emma let her hands glide over his chest. Her fingers trailed over the ridges of his muscles, weaving a long, winding pattern until she reached the waistband of his pants.

"You will rush me if you do that." Bo once again took Emma's hands, this time using one hand to pin hers gently above her head. His other hand unsnapped the button of her jeans. He kissed the skin above the waistband of her underwear, easing her jeans down her legs.

Emma tried to pull her arms away, but Bo kept her pinned. "Bo, please let me."

Releasing her, Bo caressed her legs, yanked off her boots, and peeled her socks off. He then kissed the top of one foot, then the other. Then he removed her jeans the rest of the way.

It was strangely exciting having Bo pull off her socks and kiss her feet. She wouldn't have thought it sexy but changed her mind when his mouth kissed the inside of her calf, then the inside of her thigh.

Bo pulled away and stood to pull off his own shoes and socks. When Emma sat up to unbutton his pants, this time he let her. His abdominal muscles contracted under her touch. He kicked off his pants when she pulled them down.

And when her hands caressed him from the tips of his toes to the inside of his thighs, he shuddered under them. He dropped to his knees when she bent and kissed the inside of his thigh.

Emma grabbed for Bo's last remaining garment, and he didn't stop her from removing it as he had with his shirt and pants. She looked up into his eyes as she eased his briefs down his legs.

"I imagined you here like this with me." Bo gently pushed Emma back down on the bed. He removed her underwear and simply gazed at her body.

"I couldn't tell." Emma wanted to grab the blanket while he looked at her nude body, not used to having a man see her like this. But instead, she let her eyes wander his body. She had not yet found the courage to do so.

Bo knelt between Emma's thighs, settling himself against her. He kissed her again, this time using his body to caress hers. He lost what was left of his control and concentrated on her body, touching and caressing her from the top of her head to her feet once again. His hands came back up her body, lingering and arousing.

"Bo, please." Emma could hear the breathless pleading, but she didn't care. His mouth was on her breasts again, and his hand was teasing and tormenting her. He kept his touch light, so much so that she wanted to force him closer to ease the ache that was building with each stroke of his fingers and the tender touch of his hand.

Bo lightly bit her breast, then not so lightly. Emma was more than ready for him. His touch became a little firmer, a little bolder, and she arched beneath him. When she blindly reached for him, he arched himself into her touch, savoring the feel of her fingers on him. "Do you want me, Emma?"

Emma squeezed him a little harder. "Yes, Bo, please."

Bo took her hand and opened her fingers to release him. He placed her hands on his chest, while his legs fully parted her thighs. He settled once again against her, this time probing her body, slowly entering and pulling away until she thrust her hips against his.

Emma moaned, and her fingernails dug into his chest as he took her fully. She kept her eyes on his, their color much darker in the shadows of the bed. It wasn't until he began to move slowly in and out of her that her eyes closed, and she gave herself completely to him.

Bo was sure he had not seen a more beautiful woman or had ever been so moved by the complete trust one showed him. Emma's arms left his chest and wrapped around his neck as she lifted herself into his slow thrusts, her breasts crushed to his chest. He kept his pace slow, wanting this moment with her to last.

Emma felt him caressing her inside and out, and she clung to him, her fingers gripping the muscles of his back. She wanted to beg him to move faster, to finish what he had started, but she had no words. Her thighs gripped his, and her body clenched around him. She heard him moan in her ear, then she could hear soft words that he spoke, though they were not in English. She would have smiled had she not been so focused on the feeling of him inside her.

Bo felt the desperation in her as she almost fought him for release. Releasing his control, he surged into her, increasing his movements and penetration of her. When her release came, he thrust a little further and held himself still inside her, savoring the moment. Then needing release as desperately as she did, he thrust one last time, letting himself go.

Emma relaxed her thighs but used her arms to hug him to her. She felt tears sting her eyes, and she willed them away. She didn't want to ruin the moment by getting weepy again.

"Emma." He spoke her name against her ear as he kissed the skin of her neck.

Emma smiled. "What did you say to me earlier?"

Bo took her hands from around his neck and pinned them back to the bed. He gazed down at her, remembering what he had said. They were the words of a man thoroughly enjoying what he was doing. "Let's just say they were pretty lusty."

Emma laughed and lifted her mouth to kiss him. "Next time, you should try it in English so I understand."

Bo was not sure there would be a next time, but he nodded. "I will."

Emma relaxed until Bo pulled out of her and used his strength to resettle them until she was lying on top of him. Startled, she looked down into his face, but his eyes were closed. She relaxed again, not worrying about her slighter frame crushing his much larger one.

Emma dozed for a while before once again stirring. "I should probably go home."

Bo's eyes shot open. Emma slid off him and started gathering her clothes.

"I can't find my underwear."

Bo turned on the bedside lamp to help. He found her underwear on the floor opposite the rest of their clothes. He gazed at Emma, her body glowing in the lamplight. Her breasts were bigger than her frame should have allowed; her waist was slim, and her hips flared slightly out. When she turned her back to him to pick up her pants, it occurred to him that he had barely touched her from the back. He tossed her underwear onto the bed and came toward her.

Emma was startled when Bo tugged her to her feet and against him. With her back pressed against his chest, she could feel his renewed interest. Her knees went weak as she felt her own.

"You have no idea how lovely you are to me, Emma. You make me want all the things I told myself I do not deserve."

Emma wanted to ask him what he meant but couldn't when his teeth bit the back of her neck. All thought fled. He set her partially away from him, his hands running down her back. His fingers caressed her backside, and she found herself parting her thighs for him while they stood beside the bed, her pants clutched to her chest.

"Again. And that is English." Bo came up behind her until her hands were braced against the wall. This time there was no finesse, no soft words. He used his fingers on her until she was straining against him and panting. Turning her around so he could watch her face, he lifted her until her legs were wrapped around his waist. He thrust into her, using the wall to brace her.

Emma held onto him while he took her again. She was amazed as she felt her body responding to his, her own release coming only a moment before his. Feeling dazed, her head dropped to his shoulder.

Bo settled her back on the bed. "Your cousin will sleep a while yet. As will Fan. Stay."

Emma watched as Bo set the alarm on his phone. She saw he had set it for five a.m.

Bo settled beside her. "The alarm will guarantee you will not sleep in and be home in plenty of time."

Emma settled next to him on the small bed, her head on Bo's shoulder. She sighed when he pulled the covers over them. She fell asleep with her hand over Bo's heart.

* * *

"Sleep well?" Emma greeted her cousin as she fixed breakfast. It was only 6 a.m., but farm life started early. Emma had reluctantly left Bo's bed when the alarm went off. He had helped her dress, kissed her ever so gently, then sent her on her way. She had wanted to cry because the kiss had felt more like a goodbye kiss than a good morning one.

Maryanne rubbed her low back and nodded. "It's always so peaceful here. Even with the little man here bouncing around, I got some sleep. There were times I thought I would never sleep again."

Emma came and put her hand on Maryanne's belly. "My little cousin here is just anxious to come out and see the world."

Maryanne laid a hand on top of Emma's. "It can be a rough world out there. I love him, Emma, but I am afraid for him. I never thought I'd have a child, at least not so long as I was married to Ping. Not after what I learned about him."

Emma drew away. "You could have come to me. I would have helped you. You didn't have to live through that alone."

Maryanne sat down. "I knew that in my heart. But my head told me that I had brought this on myself. I had been impulsive. I married a man I didn't know very well. He was so different from the boys I dated. He was a grown man, and he swept me off my feet. He had charm, and he had money, and he spoiled me. I fell for it. And I admit that his money was a big draw. We never had much growing up, and the thought of being with someone who did was appealing. I still wonder if that is why I married him. It shamed me. And it shamed me to know what he was and that I didn't see it. I couldn't bring that home."

"When will you leave?" Emma set a bowl of oatmeal in front of Maryanne, who grimaced.

"Oatmeal? Seriously? You know I hate oatmeal."

"It's good for you, and it's all I have right now to feed you. And you didn't answer my question."

Maryanne picked up the spoon and swirled the oats. "Soon. I don't trust Ping. He might show up just because he's mad. I want to be gone. But I need a couple of days to rest. Tomorrow I will make arrangements for Fan and me to fly home."

"And I need to pack up the house."

Maryanne looked around. "There isn't much left. The house was always full of stuff. What happened to it all?"

Emma dished up a bowl of oatmeal for herself. "Aunt Jenna took most of it when Daddy died. A lot of the stuff belonged to his side of the family. Jenna was worried about what would happen to it, and I told her to take it. I just need to pack up my clothes and a few items in my room. Sheriff Townsend said he could get a couple of local teenagers to help me move the rest of the furniture to the apartment I will be renting. That was if I didn't go with you."

"Emma, I'm sorry, really I am. I hadn't realized you were thinking of coming with me."

"It's not your fault. I've been floundering for the past few months since Dad passed. I didn't want to face the reality of the situation I was in."

They ate quietly for a while before Maryanne spoke again. "I heard you creep in this morning. Where were you?"

Emma choked on a bite of oatmeal. She kept her head down. "I was with a friend."

"That's not like you. But I guess with Fan around, you and your friend probably don't see much of each other."

Emma wanted to confide in her cousin, but something held her back. Since she left Bo's cabin, she kept thinking about what he'd said. He said she made him want things he didn't deserve. She had wanted to ask him what he meant by that, but he had easily distracted her. Once more in the night, he had reached for her, and she had gone to him willingly. It was as if he were starving, and she was a feast. Or perhaps a better analogy was that she was something he wasn't supposed to have, so he reveled in it while he had it.

She wasn't sure if she should be annoyed or flattered that she was forbidden fruit.

He had not made any promises to her last night or this morning. And while she was entertaining fantasies of something permanent between them, he'd barely spoken to her as they both dressed. He had walked her back to her door, kissed her lightly, and said nothing else before he made his way back to his cabin.

"I didn't hear the car, so it must be your tenant. How long has that been going on?"

Emma set her spoon down. Doubts assailed her for the first time. "Last night was the first time. He's been nothing but a perfect gentleman since he arrived. I'm afraid I may have pushed him into something he didn't want."

"I doubt it. I may not be an expert on men, but sex is something men generally won't turn down if offered. And it's not something you can force them into. Either they want you, or they don't."

"I suppose. I've not known him long, but I really like him."

Maryanne took Emma's hand. "You're in love with him, aren't you?"

Emma knew the answer to the question but was afraid to admit it. "Maybe. Probably."

"Well, at least he's a cop and not a human-trafficking monster like Ping. I like to think there are good men in the world, despite my marriage to Ping, and I hope yours is one of them."

The conversation came to an end when Fan joined them in the kitchen. Emma fixed her a bowl of oatmeal and tossed in raisins with some brown sugar. "Why don't you two help me in the greenhouse today? I have to load the truck up with some plants and take them to town."

"Sure. I can help some, just no heavy lifting." Maryanne ate her oatmeal while Fan chatted.

Emma finished her own and then went upstairs to change. She had taken a shower when she'd gotten back from Bo's, letting the hot water soothe her muscles and clear her head. She did some of her best thinking in the early morning hours while taking a hot shower.

Emma pulled on some fresh clothes and brushed her teeth. She glanced out her window, but Bo was not outside. He didn't work today, so perhaps he had gone back to sleep after she left. She couldn't blame him if he had gone back to bed. They had gotten to bed late, and they had awoken in the middle of the night to make love again.

Emma told herself not to romanticize what happened, but she couldn't help it. She was a bit old-fashioned. She didn't sleep around, though she had another relationship after Lonnie. He lived a few towns over, so they didn't see much of each other. Eventually, he asked her to move in with him, but she didn't want to leave her farm, and he didn't want to move in with her to what he called the boonies. After that, they drifted apart. She didn't know what happened to him, if he found someone else after her, but she hoped he had and wished him well.

Emma sighed and closed the curtains so she would stop looking for Bo. She had things to do today, and then she had things to start packing. She had boxes in the basement waiting to be filled. One truckload would move all of her things, except for the furniture. Part of her wanted to leave it all behind, start fresh somewhere else. Somewhere far away. But she couldn't do that, any more than she could somehow change the past and find a way to save her home. But things changed, and she had to change with them. With that thought in the forefront of her mind, she went to find her cousin and Fan and got on with the day.

Chapter Seven

Bo used just about every swear word he knew in both Mandarin and English as he watched Emma leave her house with Maryanne Biao in tow. At no point in their conversations had Emma told him that Maryanne was pregnant. And Bo had no doubt Biao was the father. If that baby she carried was male, that could change the whole game.

Bo remained inside the house. He didn't want Maryanne to see him. It was too risky that she might recognize him from a picture or recognize his name. The downside to being undercover using your own identity was that you could not hide behind a false identity. Everyone in the darker corners of Hong Kong knew who he was. Maryanne was part of those dark places, whether she liked it or not.

But a baby was a whole other issue. If that baby were a boy, Biao might just come back for it. He knew he would need to alert Jonas to the fact, so he would not be taken by surprise like he had just been.

Bo picked up his phone. Jonas was a couple of hours ahead of him and was probably at work by now. He dialed the number and waited.

"Twice in a week. I think that might be a record."

Jonas's voice came over the line.

Bo winced, though it was probably not Jonas's intention to remind Bo that the longer he was in the U.S., the more involved with his family he was becoming, whether he wanted to or not. "Do not get used to it. I have some news, and I do not think it is good."

That got Jonas's attention. He'd been listening to some chatter, and it was making him a bit nervous. His wife, Lian, was now permanently on staff with the FBI, and she had been listening to the recordings all morning. Bo's name had come up in some disturbing conversations. "What's up?"

Bo looked out the window again to see Emma loading her truck with trays of plants. "Maryanne Biao showed up. She is pregnant."

Jonas was quiet for a moment, gathering his thoughts. "You're right. I don't think that's good. It might be the incentive Biao needs to come back."

Bo dropped the curtain back. "He might if the child is male. I would say she has two, maybe three months left. Nothing I have heard makes me believe that Biao knows."

"But if it got leaked to him that she was, he might be lured out. I need to think about this."

Bo was not opposed to Jonas using Maryanne as bait, but he had a feeling Emma would not be as understanding. And Bo did not want to put Fan in danger. "You think. But if you think the answer is yes, you had best be prepared to protect all three of them."

"All three?"

Bo closed his eyes, seeing Emma's sweet face smiling at

him. "The cousin is not going to sit around and let you use her family to capture Biao. If you recall, the woman pulled a shotgun on a triad leader. She has guts."

Jonas had the reports from the local sheriff. "Like I said, let me think about it. I'll let you know. I do have a question for you. Have you seen anything strange? Seen anyone or heard anything out of the ordinary?"

"No. Why?"

Jonas was hesitant but knew it was probably best to warn Bo rather than have Bo take the law into his own hands or to disappear. "There was some odd chatter from some of the triad members we've been keeping under surveillance. Mostly Biao's men who scattered after Kang was killed and Biao was added to the most wanted list."

The mention of Kang got Bo's attention. Kang had been a low-level triad member under Biao. Biao had set him up, and Kang was killed during an FBI shootout. But Kang had his own men here in the States as well as Hong Kong, and it was conceivable that the men who were stateside would try to resurrect the business.

Bo answered Jonas honestly. "I have not heard anything. I have some of my contacts back in Hong Kong keeping me posted on anything of interest while I am here. As far as I know, my name has not been popping up, other than speculation on what I might be doing here in the U.S. Since my cover is still intact, I have also been in contact with my men. They are getting restless, and no doubt trying to figure out how to overthrow me, but nothing unusual there either."

"All right. Let me know if that changes. Keep your

phone with you. I'll get in touch with my superiors about Maryanne as well. If we have to bring her in, I'll need their sanction."

Bo ended the call and went back to his computer. He sent a line to his own superiors to see if they had heard any chatter. He relayed that Jonas was investigating but had no concrete evidence at this time. Bo was not concerned. His leaders within the triad would not hesitate to overthrow him while he was gone, but Bo had thwarted more than one conspirator against him over the years.

Bo also realized that now was probably not the right time to tell Jonas that Fan was their sister. The more people who knew, the greater the risk to Fan should anyone find out. Secrets could only be kept for a short time. And if Bo told Jonas, Jonas would tell his superiors. Better that Jonas take Maryanne, Emma, and Fan into custody and protect them from Biao. The FBI wanted Maryanne's testimony if they could capture Biao and get him to court. Bo did not have as much faith in the FBI as his brother did. Biao, despite the fact that his own men were now out to get him, would not be deterred from his own goals. Bo expected Biao would make an appearance eventually. The question was where.

Jonas had made it public knowledge that Biao was turning evidence for the government. Though not true, it served the FBI's purpose of keeping Biao in the U.S. so he could be caught. Should Biao set foot in Hong Kong, or any other major city in China, he would likely be assassinated. But Biao would still have followers, those who would not blindly trust what they had heard about their leader. It was those followers and those men who were protecting Biao now. They would not be easy to find.

Restless but unable to leave the house, Bo closed his laptop and went to take a long, cold shower.

* * *

"Who was the fellow at dinner the other night?"

Emma glanced up to see Lonnie standing next to her truck. She glanced around but didn't see his wife or kids. "Hi, Lonnie. Want to give me a hand with this?"

Lonnie came around and picked up a large tray of plants. "I'm serious, Em. Who is he? He's not from around here."

Emma carried a tray into the loading area and went back to her truck. "He's a police officer who moved to town a little over a month ago. He's renting my cabin."

"You two seemed pretty cozy." Lonnie climbed into the truck bed to move the larger trays to the front.

Emma paused to wipe the sweat from her brow. "He's a nice guy. And if we seem cozy, it's because we are."

Lonnie stood up and glared down at her. "He's not your type."

Emma put her hands on her hips. "You mean he's not the right color. Why don't you say what you mean?"

Lonnie jumped down. "Fine. He's not. But more importantly, he's not one of us. He's an outsider."

Feeling extremely irritated, she brushed past him and grabbed another tray of plants. "Well, he won't be an outsider anymore if I marry him."

"You can't be serious. Have you no common sense? You can't marry a man like that."

Emma ignored him and finished unloading the truck. Lonnie stood to the side watching her. When she was about to climb into her truck, he blocked her. "Get out of my way."

"Look. I'm worried about you, that's all. We go way back, and I don't want to see you taken advantage of."

"Sorry, Lonnie, you've got that backwards. I'm the one taking advantage of him. So don't worry about it. Go home to your wife and kids."

Lonnie kept himself planted against her door. "I know I hurt you. I hurt you so much that you haven't found another man. You must be desperate to take up with someone like him."

Emma wasn't sure what part of that statement was the most offensive. "You hurt me. I got over it. And there have been men since you. Get out of my way."

Lonnie went to grab her, and she elbowed him in the gut. He grunted and moved away from her door. Satisfied, she climbed in and locked the door behind her. She pulled out of the parking lot, leaving Lonnie in a cloud of exhaust. She pushed him, and the incident, out of her mind. Though it was one of the more unpleasant conversations between her and Lonnie that she'd had with him over the years, it wasn't the first unpleasant conversation they'd had.

Emma glanced over at her purse. The check inside from the nursery made selling her plants a little easier to handle. She pulled into the bank and deposited the check. The teller greeted her by name, and Emma asked her how her mother was doing. The young woman's mom had taken a tumble down some stairs and broken her arm.

The transaction finished and assured that the teller's mom was on the mend, Emma headed home. She imagined Maryanne was having a nap, as well as Fan. Emma smiled, thinking she might get a little more alone time with Bo. Now that the cat was out of the bag, so to speak, she might as well take advantage of the situation. But her mind went back again to his comment that he didn't deserve her, and the kiss that morning that seemed like a farewell rather than a hello.

She turned onto the county road that led to her home. It wasn't until she was pulling into her driveway that she noticed all the vehicles outside her house and the number of people milling about. Seeing Bo outside on his front step talking to a man dressed in a dark suit, her stomach clenched. All of the SUVs parked outside were black, and all of the men were dressed in similar attire. And they all had vests that clearly said FBI on them.

Emma stopped her truck near Bo's SUV and glanced around for Maryanne and Fan. She saw them standing a few yards away, talking to another man. Maryanne's face was tense, and Fan looked scared. Emma's first thought was that Ping had come back. She scanned all the faces but didn't see Ping's in the crowd. Somewhat relieved, she stepped out of her truck.

Bo's gut clenched as Emma started heading his way. Knowing it was the best thing for her, he turned his back on her.

Emma stopped in her tracks, the hurt sudden and deep.

Then she realized she was making a beeline for Bo when she should have been making her way to Maryanne and Fan. After seeing the cold, hard look on his face and his dismissal, she took off running toward her family.

She embraced Fan first, then Maryanne. She ignored the man who was nearby. "What happened?"

Maryanne had one arm around Fan and one around her belly. "The FBI found me. They think I stole money from Ping and that's why he came after me last year. And now they want me to go into protective custody. The man over there talking to Bo is Special Agent Jonas Cole. He's been looking for Ping for the past year."

Emma glanced over to the man talking earnestly with Bo. And something in Maryanne's tone had her on full alert. "What does Bo have to do with this?"

Maryanne scoffed. "I should have asked you the full name of your tenant. As it was, I must have been exhausted to not consider the possibility that your Bo was Ping's Bo. I just never imagined this would happen. You've been housing a triad leader in your guest cabin. Not that Agent Cole can prove it. If he could, he would be arresting your boyfriend instead of just questioning him."

"What?" Emma's knees went weak.

"Bo Lee is a triad leader out of Hong Kong. The CIA and the FBI have been trying to prove for years that he's guilty, but they don't have proof. He's bought off every cop and government official he could to keep his name clean. He took over when his father was murdered. Ping hates him, but Bo has too much power to be stopped by a bottom feeder like Ping. Bo Lee runs a multibillion-dollar company that is a front for his operation. He's the one behind the human trafficking and gun running that Ping is involved in."

Emma couldn't breathe. She glanced over at Bo, who was talking heatedly with Agent Cole. She doubled over, afraid she was going to pass out.

Maryanne took a grip on her arm, holding her until it passed. "I'm sorry, Emma. I wish I could tell you otherwise."

"I let him…" She paused, unable to get any other words out.

Maryanne put herself between the FBI agent watching them and Emma. "I know. You didn't know. It will be okay. I promise."

Emma knew she had no choice but to get herself together. She could feel Fan's hand taking hold of hers. She had to get a grip, if for no other reason than not to frighten Fan. She dropped to her knees and hugged Fan to her.

"Auntie Emma?" Fan whispered as she clutched her aunt.

Emma brushed her hair back and gave her a small smile. "I'm okay. I just got a little dizzy, is all."

Fan went back to her mother. She latched onto her when her mother picked her up. She kept her face pressed against her shoulder.

The agent standing nearby came to stand beside the women. "My name is Agent Leon Tanner. I work with Agent Cole. We are not here to hurt or arrest your cousin. We need to take her into protective custody for the sake of both her and the children. Do you understand?"

Emma understood. And she understood why the agent was being vague. She could appreciate that he was not saying anything about Ping in front of Fan. Emma nodded to the agent. Her head was pounding, and her mouth was dry. Now that the fainting spell had passed, she was more worried about throwing up.

Agent Tanner crowded the three of them and started taking them back to the house. "I need you to pack up your things. Just pack what you need into one suitcase each. We can worry about getting you anything else you might need later."

Maryanne nodded and carried Fan up the stairs.

Emma remained behind, tears stinging her eyes.

"You should pack as well, Ms. McKinnon."

Emma was startled. "Why?"

Agent Tanner had been instructed on what he should and should not say to Ms. McKinnon. "Agent Cole thinks once it becomes knowledge that Mrs. Biao and Fan are in protective custody with the FBI, Ping Biao may come after you. He may try to use you to get to your cousin. Agent Cole feels it is in your and our best interests if you come with us."

Stunned, Emma headed up the stairs. Instead of going to her room, she went to Maryanne's. She went in and closed the door behind her. Maryanne was holding Fan and trying not to cry.

"Are you going with them?" Emma came and sat beside Maryanne on the bed.

"I don't think I have a choice. Last year I managed to get away from the police. And look what happened to me.

Agent Cole thinks that because of the baby, Ping is likely to hunt me down, no matter where I go. I got the impression that Agent Cole was not against simply arresting me and forcing my cooperation. If that happens, what will happen to Fan?"

Emma knew Maryanne was scared for both of her children. "Agent Tanner seems nice."

Maryanne gave a watery laugh. "For a cop. I suppose I should be grateful they're willing to protect me for my testimony as opposed to arresting and coercing me to cooperate. But either way, they get what they want."

Emma pulled out Fan's suitcase from the closet and started packing it herself. Maryanne looked shell-shocked. Emma was feeling much the same, but the activity at least gave her a purpose. Thoughts of Bo and last night were bombarding her, and she wanted to scream at the injustice of what had happened. Emma had a feeling what she was feeling at this moment was the same thing Maryanne felt when she realized what her husband was. Emma had wondered how Maryanne hadn't known before she married him. Now she knew.

Maryanne got herself together and instructed Fan to gather up the toys she wanted to bring. She then came and pulled the suitcase from Emma's hands. "Let me finish. You should pack your bag."

Emma numbly went to her bedroom. She pulled an old, worn suitcase from the closet. It had belonged to her father. He had used it when he went to medical seminars. Her parents had never traveled, never had the money to. This suitcase had been bought secondhand at a thrift store in town. Wiping tears she wasn't aware she was shedding, she set the case on the bed and started tossing clothing inside. She didn't know where they would go or what she would need. She grabbed her toiletries from the bathroom and packed what little jewelry she had. She had an anniversary ring her father had given her mother years ago. She also had a necklace that belonged to her grandmother.

She then picked up a ring she hadn't worn in years. It was a promise ring Lonnie had given her when they were seniors. Though they had been officially engaged, they had not gotten around to buying rings. Emma set it on the dresser, not wanting to bring along a reminder of a broken promise. She then grabbed the family portrait hanging on her bedroom wall, wrapped it in some clothes, and zipped the suitcase up.

Emma glanced around, but there was nothing else to take. She picked up the suitcase and carried it downstairs to wait for Maryanne and Fan. Agent Tanner was standing near the front door. She didn't speak to him but walked to the front window of her living room. From her view of the front yard, she could see that many of the agents were simply waiting and watching for trouble. She looked at the cabin, but Bo was not there. Both he and Agent Cole were gone. Bo's SUV was parked outside, but Emma imagined Bo was now being escorted to wherever it was that the local FBI used for interrogation.

She set her suitcase down near the front door. She then went to the kitchen and emptied out the coffee container, dumping the grounds in the trash. She then went to Agent Tanner. He didn't step away from the door to let her pass.

"I have to go get something from the greenhouse."

Agent Tanner gestured to another agent to take Emma to the greenhouse.

She took the distance between the house and the greenhouse at a slow pace. She took the time to get herself back under control. A deep anger was starting to take root. She only had a few days left in her home, and she was being forced to abandon it. Emma had no idea what would happen to the rest of her things; she doubted she was going to get the opportunity to find out. She took the coffee can and went to where she stored her most prized possessions. She tucked various flower seeds carefully into the can before sealing the lid onto the can with some twine.

On her way out of the greenhouse, she glanced up to see the bright petals of her hibiscus. China roses, Bo had called them. Her eyes filled with tears until they were just a bright pink blur.

Chapter Eight

Bo paced the hotel room where he was hiding. Jonas was finishing up a phone call. He had seriously considered disappearing but figured getting himself added to the list of people Jonas was tracking was not worth it. He did not want Jonas to waste his resources tracking him down when he should be focusing on finding Biao.

Jonas hung up and watched his brother pace. "I got a name."

Bo stopped. Jonas had shown up unexpectedly at Emma's home. At first, Bo had been angry. His first thought was that he never should have told Jonas where he was. Well, to be fair, his first thought had been Emma and that his brief happiness had come to an end. There was no way to explain to her who he was, why he was there, or that she shouldn't believe all the things she was going to hear about him.

Bo was surprised by how hard it was to keep his emotions in check. He had learned the hard way not to let softer emotions rule his life. That way led to disaster.

Bo dropped into a chair. "Run it by me again. You showed up today because you think someone is going to attempt to kill me?"

Jonas couldn't get a read on his brother. Since he had

shown up earlier in the day, Bo had been even more uncommunicative than he normally was. "Fine. Lian has been listening to a lot of chatter going on with several triad members who still claim allegiance to Biao. It would seem Biao has taken the time he's been in hiding to gather as much intel about you as he could. He claims to have proof you're a cop. He took that proof to the man who is now hunting you."

Bo figured there were only two men, besides Biao, who would turn on him given enough evidence. "Who?"

"A man named Feng Wong."

Bo's laughter was harsh. "He would be my first choice. My number one."

Jonas looked confused. "I thought Biao was your number one."

Bo shook his head. "Number two, though he was number one when my father was alive."

Jonas automatically corrected him. "Our father. Do you think the evidence Biao has is enough to prove you're a cop?"

"Feng would not need much in the way of evidence to believe I was a cop. My other number one, now he would require a significant amount of evidence to be convinced of my being a crook. He's convinced that the rumors about me are just that."

"Your other number one?" Jonas poured himself a cup of coffee. It was going to be a long night.

"Feng is my triad number one. My other number one is an American by the name of Josh Lanford. He is my vice president. I have been grooming him to take over the company. Or at least the legitimate parts."

"So Lanford doesn't know you're a cop, but thinks you're a good guy?"

"Yes. He and I worked very closely while my father was still alive. He knew Howard for what he was, and I used him from time to time to feed information to the police. Josh believes he was simply aiding in an investigation I was cooperating with."

"How dangerous is Feng to your cover?"

Bo thought about it for a moment. "Feng could come up with enough evidence to convince a jury I was guilty of several heinous crimes. But if he were to find out I am a cop, he might very well come hunt me himself, no matter where I might be. If he can convince the rest of my men I am a cop, I will not be safe anywhere."

Jonas swore. "Right now, Feng has issued a reward of ten million dollars for your head."

Bo gave another harsh laugh. "Is that all?"

"This isn't funny. You have a number of men looking to kill you."

Bo shrugged. "It has been that way my whole life. This is not the first time I have had a price on my head, but it is the first time because I was a cop. I have a feeling my being a cop will be a bigger motivation to kill me than money. Feng and the other men will make it their mission to kill a traitor in their ranks."

Jonas had a feeling Bo was right. "I need you to be straight with me, Bo. I can't help you if you keep on keeping your secrets."

"Sometimes keeping secrets is the safest thing for

everyone around you."

Jonas slammed his palm on the table. "You need my help. If you don't want the help of the FBI, then at least accept the help of your older brother instead."

Bo rubbed his eyes, fatigue weighing on him. "I think you have missed the most important piece of this situation."

Jonas sat, too, just as weary. "And what is that?"

Bo looked up to watch his brother's face, hoping to frighten him enough so he would turn his back on him instead of insisting on helping him. "Feng will hunt me. If he finds me and kills me, who do you think is next? Biao knows you are my brother. Feng would know what Biao knows. And when he is done with you, he will go after your pretty wife. And do not forget about your mother. He will go after her, too. After all, she murdered his previous leader and mothered the current one that betrayed him."

Jonas paled but stood his ground. "Which is why you need to cooperate with me instead of fighting me at every turn. Help me find Biao and help me find Feng before he finds you. The price on your head didn't specify the reason. It's possible only Biao and Feng know you're a cop. Why would Feng keep that a secret?"

Bo was not surprised Jonas was even more determined to help him. He sighed and relented. "Feng may not want to stir up the ranks just yet. It could be he wants to be absolutely sure before he tells anyone. It would not look good on him for others to know he had been answering to a cop this whole time and did not know. Like I have always said, it is hard to keep secrets. There is no telling what would happen if it became common knowledge I am a cop.

If I were a low-level informant, it would be one thing. But you are talking about their leader, the man they look to, and for some, the man they look up to. If it were even rumored the cops were that close to the top of the triad, rival triads might try to take the whole clan out. There could be rebellion in the ranks as well. So, for now, Feng might keep his secrets. Most likely the reason he is giving my men for hunting me is that I have abandoned them. It is time for new blood."

Jonas digested that. It made sense. "That works to our benefit. Then I have to only worry about Feng and Biao. But I also need to make sure you're safe from the thugs who would gain from your death. Once we have both men in custody, maybe I can sleep again. Maybe we both can."

Bo changed the subject. Since he had last laid eyes on Emma, she was what he wanted to know about. "What did you tell Maryanne and Emma about me?"

"Nothing yet. Tanner talked with them. Maryanne told Emma you are a triad leader, and that Biao works for you. Both women came without argument. Maryanne fears for her children. I don't know what motivates Ms. McKinnon, except fear for her family. Tanner was given strict instructions not to blow your cover. He is only one of two agents, besides myself and my superiors, who know who you really are."

"Good. The less of the truth they know, the better. I trust they are in good hands?"

"They are."

Both men were silent for a while, then Jonas rose. "I have to go. Maryanne Biao has evidence we need to convict her husband. My superiors are none too happy that I am using taxpayers' money to protect Ms. McKinnon. We both know it is highly unlikely Biao will go after her when he knows we have his wife in custody. Ms. McKinnon doesn't have any value to him. Want to tell me the real reason you're worried about her before I leave?"

Bo could not tell his brother that it was more for his benefit than hers. But Bo could not help but feel that if Emma were available, Biao would find a way to use her as leverage. Biao may not be able to use Emma as a negotiation tool with the FBI, but she could be used to manipulate Maryanne. And for that reason alone, he wanted her safely in FBI custody.

Bo shook his head. "Call it a hunch."

"I'll be sure to tell that to my superiors."

Bo dropped his head in his hands when Jonas slammed the door behind him. He knew that if he got too close, he would hurt Emma. And now he had hurt her in the worst way possible.

Bo rose and poured himself a cup of coffee. He needed to think. And Bo needed a plan in case Jonas was unable to find Feng and Biao before they found him.

* * *

"Am I going to be arrested?" Emma asked Agent Cole the question that was most pressing on her mind. Since she had arrived home to find the FBI on her doorstep, she had been in a fog. Once the initial hurt and tears passed, they left behind a deep-seated anger in their place. Then came fear.

"Now why would I do that, Ms. McKinnon?" Jonas took a seat across from the lovely young woman whose eyes held his. Her sun-streaked blonde hair was a bit tangled around her face, and her eyes were very blue, though at the moment more red than blue from tears.

"I was housing a triad leader. Seems like grounds for an arrest."

"Emma. You are not going to be arrested for housing Bo Lee. You had no way of knowing who he was. His cover was sound."

Relief crashed through her and allowed the anger to come back to the forefront. "Maryanne told me who he was. I thought he was a cop. So did our sheriff. I thought he was a good guy. I let him in my home. I let him near my niece. What if he had hurt her? What if he had gotten away with using her and Maryanne to lure out Ping? They could have been killed."

Jonas tried to stem her hysteria. "We have no reason to believe Bo was there to harm the child or you."

"Then why?" Emma heard the shrillness in her voice but couldn't help it.

Jonas took her hand and patted it. "We think he was simply scoping the place out. Though it was not a likely scenario that Biao would show up in person, Bo could have simply come to get information from Mrs. Biao."

Emma looked at him in disbelief. "You can't seriously believe that I had a triad leader in my home hoping to just 'get information.'"

He knew it was a long shot, and obviously Emma

McKinnon wasn't going to buy his story. "Ok. Truth is we don't know exactly why he was there, though we have theories. But we did know he was there, so that should give you some comfort. We have been keeping an eye on him for some time, and he knew it. Should anything have happened to you or your cousins, he would have been our first suspect. The first thing you should know about Bo is that he keeps his hands clean. It's why he's not in custody."

Emma couldn't help but wonder what the man in front of her would think if she told him the whole truth about her relationship with Bo. The man before her had the same color hair as Bo and had a similar build, though he was taller. His dark brown eyes were piercing, though she was sure they held a bit of compassion in them. She supposed it was a testament to the type of man he was that, given his age and status with the FBI, he had any compassion left.

"How long do you think we'll have to stay hidden? My cousin is pregnant. The stress can't be good for her."

Jonas wished he could give her the answer she wanted, but he couldn't make promises. "Biao has been able to avoid arrest throughout his varied career. The FBI has been looking for him for some time. And while we have some leads, I can't be sure how long it will take to flush him out."

"Don't some people stay in custody their whole lives?"

"Sometimes. But it shouldn't come to that. Maryanne told Agent Tanner she was planning to go back to China. She wouldn't be safer there. Biao has men there as well as here. Trust me when I say she is safer with us. And so are you."

"I don't see why Biao would come after me unless he

thought I could lead him to Maryanne. I guess I don't know why Biao would care. We both told Agent Tanner that Maryanne doesn't have Biao's money. The money she had came from me, and that money came from my father's life insurance policy when he died."

Jonas didn't hold back. "The baby Maryanne is carrying is all the reason why Biao might come back. She is having his son. That baby is Biao's legacy."

Emma was quiet, then turned worried eyes to Jonas. "Maryanne didn't tell him. Does he know?"

"We don't know either way. But a male child could lure him out."

Emma contemplated the agent. "Maryanne might cooperate with you if your plan is to use the baby to lure him out. Until Ping is dead, she will never be completely safe. Neither would her son if Ping knew of his existence."

"I have discussed it with her. She is willing. But what about you, Ms. McKinnon? I have learned over the years that some people will do anything to protect their family. I have concerns because you didn't hesitate to pull a gun on a triad leader who was threatening your cousin. And while I can applaud the effort, I can't have you in the way."

Emma was taken aback by his firm tone, realizing for the first time how he had been tempering his speech so as not to alarm her.

Jonas didn't give her a chance to respond. "I can promise you we will keep your cousins safe. And you, as well."

Emma cleared her throat. "You said you didn't think Biao would come after me. Do you think Bo will?"

Jonas wasn't expecting the question. "You were just a convenient way for him to get close to Maryanne or Biao."

Emma's stomach clenched when she thought again about her last night with Bo. How could he have fooled her so completely? Why would he have bothered to even attempt to keep his distance from her? "He seemed so sincere."

The words were soft, but Jonas heard them. "Did something happen between you and Mr. Lee?"

Jonas's compassionate tone broke her. She began sobbing into her hands.

Jonas rose and put a comforting arm around her. Between sobs, he heard something about a greenhouse, dinner, and spending the night with him. Figuring anger was useless, he simply held Emma while she cried. Bo had not mentioned the part where he had taken the pretty witness to Biao's attack on Maryanne to bed.

Jonas heard the door open and close behind him and looked up to see Lian. His wife was frowning at him. He let Lian take his place.

"Here, Emma. You need something to drink and food in your system before you collapse." Lian handed a couple of tissues to Emma and held a water bottle to her lips to get her to take a drink.

Emma hiccupped, then swallowed the water. She then took the bottle and drained half of it.

"There you go." Lian wiped Emma's loose hair from her damp cheeks and handed her some tissues.

"Thank you." Emma wiped her eyes and discreetly blew her nose.

"My name is Lian. I work for the FBI. The scowling man behind us is my husband. I have been helping on the case to find Biao. I just got back from talking to your cousin. She's a very brave woman to have lived through what she has. From what I hear from her, you are a strong woman yourself."

Emma sniffled and took a deep breath. "I'm just a farmer. Nothing more. Can I go back to Maryanne and Fan now? I don't know where to find Biao or Bo."

Lian looked at her husband. A silent message passed between them.

"I'll have you brought back to the safe house. Let me get Agent Ardell to escort you. She is also assigned to the case."

Jonas followed Lian from the room. He was not surprised when Lian spun around to face him.

"He's gone too far this time."

"Agreed. I'll talk to him. Just don't expect miracles."

Lian followed Jonas back to the offices and waited to sit until she saw Jonas had grabbed his coat and weapon. Once he was out of sight, she got back to work. She had a lot to do if she was going to save Bo's stubborn hide, though right now she was more inclined to let Feng have him.

* * *

Jonas slammed into Bo's hotel room. "As usual, you have left out an important component of your story. When were you going to tell me that you slept with Emma McKinnon?"

Bo's hands were fisted at his sides. Trust sweet, innocent Emma to have told the FBI the whole truth, no matter how humiliating or embarrassing it would have been for her. Instead of cursing, he spoke calmly. "It did not seem relevant."

"Not relevant? I had a witness sobbing her heart out in interrogation because of you, and you didn't think it was relevant?"

Bo's gut clenched. Unable to keep up the pretense, he turned from his brother. "I am sorry."

It was Bo's tone more than his words that got Jonas's attention. "This is a real mess, you know."

His eyes filled with genuine sorrow as he turned back to Jonas. "I had not meant to touch her. I knew nothing but hurt would come of it."

"Then why did you?" Jonas's tone softened, but only a touch.

"Because I was weak. I wanted what she offered more than I wanted my next breath."

Jonas crossed to his brother and looked out the window, just as his brother was. "Sex can be gotten from any number of women if you take the time to look."

Bo rested his forehead on the glass. "It was not sex that she offered that I could not resist. It was her heart. But I should have resisted her body."

"Lian would probably kick me in my shins if she knew I was telling you this, but I couldn't resist her heart or her body. And she couldn't resist either of mine."

"You are not a criminal. There was no risk."

"No, in the end, there was no risk. But I thought there

was for a time. Didn't stop me, though."

"I should have been able to stop. I did not want to. I have no other excuse."

Jonas dropped into a nearby chair. "Happen to you a lot? Women giving you their hearts, I mean?"

Bo was not amused. "No, women do not give me their hearts. Perhaps that is why I have been declining their bodies."

That got Jonas's immediate attention. "No sex at all?"

Bo was reluctantly amused at his brother's tone. "I am not a virgin, if that is what you are asking me."

Jonas contemplated his brother. "Okay, then how long? Not including Emma."

"A few years."

"Years? Plural?"

Bo shrugged. "Think of it as self-imposed celibacy. I got tired of having to watch my back every time I climbed out of a woman's bed."

Jonas realized that his brother was dead serious. Bo might be a cop, but few knew that. He stopped and thought about what type of woman the triad leader Bo might have dated. It made him cold. "I think I actually get that."

Bo nodded. "You cannot tell anyone about what happened between us. And you need to keep Emma's mouth closed as well. Should anyone think she could be used to get to me, they would not hesitate to use her."

"You're thinking about Feng. Emma confessed in an interrogation room, but most of what she said was so jumbled it would be hard to understand her in the recording. I could barely make out what she was saying, and I was holding her. Only Lian and I know."

Bo frowned. "Lian knows?"

"She wanted me to come here and tear a few strips off you. She may have a go at you herself if she finds out where you are. Sympathy for her fellow woman."

Bo turned and leaned his back against the glass, his legs stretched out before him. "What are you going to do?"

Jonas had been asking himself that same question on the way over. He didn't have an answer. "There are two options. I kept who you are from her and everyone else. That keeps your cover intact unless this Feng character starts spreading what he knows to others. Or I can tell Emma and put her at risk should anyone else find out she knows you and uses her against you. Assuming, of course, that she could be used against you to begin with. You said she gave you her heart, but you skipped the part where you gave her yours."

"I did not skip over that part. I do not have a heart to give her. Your best option is to keep my secrets from her. Nothing good will come of her knowing the truth. The lies are kinder."

Jonas turned and mimicked Bo's stance. "I try to imagine what it must have been like for you growing up. My childhood wasn't a walk in the park, but I can't help but feel that it was a breeze compared to what you lived through and are still living through."

Bo scowled. "Some would say I had a very privileged childhood. I went to good schools, lived in what most would consider a mansion, and I had everything a young boy could want."

"And you were raised by a sadistic father who tortured our mother and countless other women and children. I shudder to think about what you endured at his hands when you displeased him."

What was past could not be changed. "Mostly he ignored me, except when it suited him to acknowledge me. When I was born, I was given Naiwen's last name instead of his. Should I not have lived up to his standards, I would have been given away or gotten rid of. But he was mostly pleased with me. Until I was older and woke up to the reality in front of me, I was the son he wanted me to be."

"What do you mean?" Jonas felt he was always chasing answers when it came to Bo.

"It does not matter. Let's just say that before I became a cop, my life would not have passed inspection. I was as bad as any other man under his command."

"You never said what made you become a cop."

"And now is not the time to tell you. I woke up, as I said. Leave it at that."

Both men were quiet for a time. Jonas kicked up to his feet and collected his jacket and weapon. "I think you may be right to keep from Ms. McKinnon who you are. You are right that other than peace of mind that she did not sleep with a human-trafficking, gun-running scumbag, she is better off with the lies. At least I will concede that it is what is best for now. I never make promises I can't keep."

Bo dipped his head. "It is one of the things we have in common."

Jonas went to the door but stopped before opening it. He turned his head to look back at his brother. "One thing you are wrong about."

"Just one?"

Jonas ignored the comment. "You do have a heart. It might be scarred and damaged, but it's there. Otherwise, you would not care about how much you hurt Emma."

Bo did not say a word as he watched his brother leave the hotel room.

Chapter Nine

Emma looked out the bedroom window of the safe house. There had been stirrings all morning among the men who were guarding them. One agent, Agent Tanner, who had been with them since day one, seemed particularly tense. Part of Emma wanted to pretend she hadn't noticed and climb back into bed until this was all over. The other part wanted to confront him and demand answers.

"What do you think they are worried about?" Maryanne rubbed her lower back as she sat on the edge of the twin bed in the bedroom Emma was using.

Emma turned to her cousin. She was not surprised Maryanne's thoughts were much like her own. But Emma didn't want to upset Maryanne any more than she already was. "Probably that baby. He's due any day. I think Agent Tanner is terrified of having to deliver the baby himself."

Maryanne smiled at that. "What do you think of him?"

"Tanner?" Emma came and sat beside her cousin. She had seen Maryanne watching him. Of course, Emma had seen Agent Tanner looking at her cousin. One would think the agent would be looking the other way given the fact that another man's baby, a criminal's baby at that, was growing inside her. But that was not the case. The man was ever attentive and had even gone shopping to prepare for the upcoming arrival of the baby.

Emma wasn't sure she should be encouraging her cousin. Then again, she wasn't sure she should discourage her either. Emma opted for the truth. "I suppose I like him well enough. He has been making our confinement easier for all of us. And Fan likes him."

Maryanne wiped the tears from her cheeks. "He was so sweet to have bought Fan a new doll for her birthday. Fan carries that doll everywhere. I just don't understand him."

Emma grabbed a tissue and handed it to her cousin. "He likes you."

Maryanne rose on a short burst of energy. "But why? I'm the wife of a criminal. Fan is the daughter of one. I'm pregnant, for Pete's sake. But he's been so sweet. Last night he rubbed my feet. What kind of man does that?"

Emma took her cousin's hand and pulled her back down to sit. Agent Tanner was always careful to keep his distance from Maryanne, so even a foot rub, however innocent, caught Emma's attention. Emma went with her heart and answered her cousin honestly. "Maybe because he sees the good in you. Just because you married Ping doesn't mean you are like him. Fan and this baby won't be like him because they'll have you as their mother. Maybe when all this is over, you should think about what a man like Agent Tanner can offer you."

"I sometimes think about what my life might have been like right now if I had never met Ping. I know it sounds crazy, but I don't wish I hadn't met him. I wouldn't have Fan or this baby. And I know it sounds crazy, too, but I want this baby, and if that means Ping had to happen, then so be it."

Emma hugged her cousin to her. "It doesn't sound crazy. Agent Cole is working very hard to track Ping down. Once he's in custody, you can file for divorce and get on with your life."

Maryanne leaned on her cousin. "I guess my biggest regret is bringing this into your life. For bringing Bo Lee into your life."

Emma's gut clenched at the mention of Bo. Emma, as hard as she tried, couldn't wipe the memory of him, the memory of his touch, from her mind. She still spent many a night crying over her foolishness. And as the weeks passed into months, the consequences of her foolishness were becoming known. It was only a matter of time before she had to say something.

Maryanne continued. "Until Ping is found, I guess it doesn't really matter. This baby is coming any day, and once the baby and I are out of the hospital, we'll be moved again."

Emma gently eased her cousin down. "You need to rest. We'll worry about that later."

Maryanne's eyes closed. "I just want this over."

Emma brushed Maryanne's hair back and waited until her cousin slept. She then quietly left the room.

Agent Cole had visited them a couple of days earlier. He told them he wanted to move them. There was a safe house in Virginia, not that far from the offices where Agent Cole worked. Agent Cole wanted them there. He hadn't said a whole lot about it other than it was better to be closer so that his own people could watch over them, and to be nearby in case they caught Ping. Agent Cole didn't want anything to go wrong once they apprehended Ping, and keeping his key witness close was his next move. What bothered Emma was that Agent Cole could have moved them weeks ago. This sudden urge to move them now made her nervous. And Emma was sure Agent Tanner knew something he wasn't telling them.

Emma went in search of the agent. Of course, he was not hard to find in the small house. He was sitting at the small table in the kitchen with a cup of coffee.

Tanner glanced up and smiled at Emma. "Maryanne resting?"

Emma went about making herself a cup of tea. "Sound asleep. The stress is getting to her. And you're not making it easier."

"Excuse me?" Tanner set his coffee down and focused on Emma.

"You heard me. First, because you're getting too close to her. The last man she let get close to her is a triad member and treated her abominably. But she's an optimist at heart and still believes that there are good men out there. But she doesn't think she deserves one. Your attention is making her edgy."

Tanner didn't dispute her words. "She does deserve a good man. I may not be the best, but I want to be there for her, take care of her."

Emma dropped into the kitchen chair opposite him. "I can see that. And I believe you. But she's married, she's scared, and she's not ready. You need to give her time and space if you want a shot with her once she's not ready to give birth to another man's baby."

"You know why I'm drawn to her?"

Emma shook her head.

Tanner looked Emma right in the eyes. "She's strong. She hasn't broken. She's seen and been forced into a life no one should have to endure. And yet she rocks Fan in her arms while Fan falls asleep. She took in another man's child as her own and loves her as her own. She loves that baby inside her, despite the father. She loves. I guess I want some of that for myself."

Emma couldn't help but be moved by Agent Tanner's sincerity.

Tanner leaned back in his seat. "What's the second reason?"

Emma's hands gripped her mug. "You're not telling us something. I don't believe for a moment that Agent Cole has just up and decided that we need to be in Virginia. Something's going on. You're tense. The other agents who come and go are also tense. They are on high alert. I told Maryanne it's simply because everyone is nervous about the baby coming, but I don't believe that."

"Agent Cole generally says what he means."

"I bet he does. But I also believe he doesn't tell the whole story. I want to know."

Tanner finished his coffee. Then coming to a decision, he sighed. "Things are complicated. Biao is still in hiding. But we've got a new player. Bo Lee's number one has shown up."

Emma had to swallow the bile that threatened to rise up. She couldn't bring herself to say his name. "His number one?"

"Look, Emma, you know Bo Lee is a triad leader. He's not at the top of the food chain, but he's up there. But he's in hiding, and his men are getting anxious. There are all sorts of rumors floating around. This man, a man named Feng Wong, is hunting him. It complicates things. Biao is not a fan of Bo's. He's been trying to take him down for years, and Bo's father before him. There's dissent among the ranks. Agent Cole thinks Feng and Biao might team up to take Bo down. Needless to say, no one wants that to happen. Biao has contacts here that Feng could use to cement his overseas business. Then taking out Bo Lee allows him to take over as head of the triad. Feng could become a very dangerous man very quickly."

"You think Feng might use Maryanne to lure out Biao so he can use him to get to Bo?" Emma could barely get the words out.

"It's a very real possibility. So now we have Biao, Bo, and Feng running loose. Agent Cole wants to make sure all four of you are safe. Moving you closer to headquarters is one way to help him do that."

Suddenly ill, Emma dashed from the kitchen to the bathroom. She barely heard Tanner knocking on the bathroom door as she sat on her knees and retched over the toilet. She got to her feet, rinsed out her mouth, and opened the door once the dizziness passed.

"I think it's past time you admitted the truth to me, if not to your cousin. How far along are you?"

Emma slid to the floor, her legs weak. "How did you know?"

Tanner crouched down in front of her. "I have ten nieces and nephews. Let's just say I recognize the signs. You're pale when you come to breakfast, you pick at your food, I've heard you crying in the night, and you've stopped drinking coffee."

"A couple of months. But don't tell her."

Tanner held out a hand and helped Emma to her feet. "I won't. Right now, she doesn't need the stress, but you'll have to tell her soon. And we'll need to make you an appointment. Once we're back in Virginia, we'll have some fresh new identities for you, and we'll get you seen."

Emma took a seat at the table and Agent Tanner left her alone. Every time someone mentioned Bo, her stomach clenched. Emma wasn't sure how she was going to get through the next few months. It wasn't as if Bo would find out she was having his baby.

The worst part was that she didn't want to believe Bo was a criminal. She had been told in great detail the type of man he was, but it was so hard to reconcile what she had been told with the man who had made love to her. The man who had helped her in her greenhouse; the man who loved China roses. It was even harder to accept because he could have pressed his advantage at any time, and yet he had kept his distance from her. He seemed to care, though reluctantly. How could she believe that a man who had been so kind and tender to her was the leader of a criminal organization?

Then there was the other part of her. The part of her that wondered if this was what Maryanne had gone through in the early days of her marriage. Had she not wanted to believe what she had seen or believe what she had been told by others? And once she knew she was pregnant, had it made it even harder to believe? Emma had not questioned Maryanne much about her relationship with Ping. And she wouldn't now. All Emma could do was pray this ended, and soon. And she prayed that Biao and Bo, and now Feng, would all be locked away for good.

* * *

"You are the most incredibly stubborn human being I know." Jonas paced the small hotel room.

Bo could almost find humor in that. "Just because I will not let you put me in protective custody does not mean I am stubborn. I do not need your protection. You just keep your men where they are now, and that is guarding Emma and her family."

"Feng is after you. Biao surfaced briefly and not near your Emma. Feng is gathering men to hunt you. Eventually, he will find you."

Bo laughed, but it lacked all humor. "I look forward to it."

Jonas slammed his hand on the table. "And then what, you kill him? What ultimate good would that do? I don't want to have to arrest you, but I will, and you know it. You need to lie low and let the FBI handle this."

Bo wished, not for the first time, that his brother was not a cop. "I helped make him what he is. All the dominoes were lining up back in Hong Kong when you got involved. Biao was making his move with Kang's help; Feng was gathering up guns and money to start a war. The police were only a couple of weeks from moving in. While Kang might be dead, Biao is still on the loose, and Feng is still going to have his war after he finds and kills me. When Feng gets rid of me, he will go back to Hong Kong, Biao should follow, and Maryanne will be safe, provided she gets the new identity you promised her, and Emma can go with her. What I started back home can finally be finished."

Jonas stopped dead in his tracks. "What do you mean once Feng gets rid of you, he'll go back to Hong Kong?"

Bo rubbed his brow, feeling the weight of all that he had been living with for the past few years draining him. "I have been thinking about my death. Right now, I am what keeps Biao here. I am what brought Feng here. I want them out of this country and away from you, Lian, your mother, and Emma. Right now, I am the link. With me gone, that link will be broken."

Jonas didn't like the look on Bo's face. "Now you listen to me. Death is not an option. Death is what happens when you lose."

Bo threw up his hands, his voice deepening. "Does this look like winning to you?"

Jonas took his brother by his shoulders. "Yes, sometimes this is what winning looks like. Sometimes it's slow. And sometimes things don't go as planned. But you don't just give up."

Bo shook off Jonas. "I told you before I am already dead. It is just a matter of time. I cannot go back to Hong Kong. It would do more harm than good at this point. My superiors have suspended me in absentia. If I go back, I would have no authority behind me. If I take out Feng, then the next man takes over, and the police will have to rebuild their case. Let Biao and Feng go back to Hong Kong. Then it will be over. At least my part."

Jonas contemplated his brother. "Actually, you might have a point."

Bo laughed, the sound harsh. "So let me do what I need to do. I can end this."

"Sit down, Brother; I have a counterproposal for you."

Bo sat and listened.

Twenty minutes later, Bo shook his head, a small curl of what he thought might be hope taking root. "I think your plan might actually work."

Jonas pulled out his phone. "I'll have to go over it with my superiors, but I think it will work."

"What will you tell Lian and your mother?"

Jonas automatically corrected him. "Our mother. I won't be able to tell her anything. This has to look real. There can't be anyone who cares about you who still thinks you're alive."

"Lian will know, yes?"

Jonas lifted his head from the message he was typing. "Yes, Lian will know. She's been helping with the investigation. But Naiwen, Griffith, and anyone else you know will need to believe you're dead."

And Emma, Bo thought. Not that she would care. She would probably find relief in the knowledge that he was dead. He rubbed the ache in his chest. "Then I suggest you get moving."

Jonas hit send and looked at his brother. "Are you

going to be able to do this? I know you think death is the best route, but you'll be leaving behind a multibillion-dollar company and your home. The government will have a blast confiscating everything you've ever owned. You will have nothing left."

He had nothing left now but did not say so. "The business will be in good hands. I already have plans in place should I die. And it is not like there is anything else there for me. I do not even have a job anymore. The suspension is just the first step before termination."

"I've been thinking about that, too. It took some digging, but you were feeding a lot of information to the CIA, as well as the Hong Kong police. I can't prove it, but I think you were more than a cop. Ever think about working for the FBI?"

"Work for you? I think not." Bo smiled, his first real smile in weeks.

"Lian could put you to work translating some of the chatter. I think she'd enjoy bossing you around."

"Of that, I have no doubt. So now what do we do?"

Jonas pulled out his handcuffs. "I arrest you."

Twenty-four hours later, Bo sat inside a secured room at the FBI headquarters. Though not a cell, it might as well be one. But he had agreed to the plan, so now he was stuck. He sat stretched out on a couch, watching the news of his arrest. It was a big day for the FBI, arresting triad leader Bo Lee on American soil. Bo had to admit his brother looked good on camera, saying that today was a win for the FBI and for all the people who had suffered at his hands. Bo was impressed, and oddly amused, to hear his brother bashing his name in the press. Of course, Bo Lee had only a few short days left to live. He could not wait to watch that report.

Bo switched off the television, closed his eyes, and tried to clear his mind. As always, once his eyes were closed, his mind drifted to Emma. Every day the ache in his gut intensified when he thought of her and of what she must be going through. And knowing she was safer this way, knowing he could not be what she needed him to be, still did not make losing her any easier.

A soft, feminine voice startled him. Bo looked up to see his sister-in-law.

"Thought you might like some company. Jonas is still fielding questions from the press."

Bo sat up and gestured to the couch. "I was watching the press conference."

Lian tucked her legs under her. "I know how strange it is to watch yourself being talked about on the news. It is a bit unsettling."

Bo never forgot what Lian had lived through. It was just one more layer of guilt that lay on his shoulders. His mother, Naiwen, had killed his father, Howard, when Howard attacked Lian. He would have raped and killed her had Naiwen not intervened. But it had been Bo, playing the grieving son, who had demanded Naiwen's and Lian's arrest. He had demanded justice. Nothing would have come of it, of course, but Lian had not known that, nor had Naiwen. Bo would be forever grateful to Griffith Dunn, a former CIA agent and now Naiwen's husband, for putting them both into hiding. He could imagine Lian and Naiwen, huddled in a safe house somewhere, watching as he railed against the injustice of what had happened and demanding they be found.

"You are a strong woman, Lian. You would need to be to survive what you did. And to find happiness. I do not think my brother knows how lucky he is."

Lian was startled by the personal comment. Bo was normally quiet around her. "I like to remind him from time to time how lucky he is. But strength is something we all have inside us. We just have to push through the fear to find it. I don't think you give yourself enough credit. You have done so much good."

Bo briefly touched Lian's cheek. "What good I have done does not outweigh the bad. I could not make up for it given two lifetimes. But this is Jonas's plan, and I have decided that perhaps his way is the cleanest for everyone."

Lian switched to Mandarin, her tone soft. "Jonas cares about you. He hates to see you suffer. I hate to see you suffer."

Bo did not have a response to that, so he remained quiet.

Lian, frustrated with him, changed her tone. "What about Emma? What are you going to do when this is over? Jonas will give you a new identity. Tanner says she still cries over you. Why don't you do the decent thing and tell her the truth?"

Bo answered in Mandarin. "So much for compassion, Sister. Emma will get over it, over me. Everyone will be safer once I am dead. Naiwen and Griffith will not have to worry about what troubles I might bring down on them because of her being my birth mother. Jonas will not have to admit I was his brother, at least publicly. Feng and Biao will be neutralized back in Hong Kong, and those who would take their place will not care a bit about me or those whom I may have cared for. I do not have children to worry about, so Bo Lee can leave this world, and it will be a better place for it."

Lian switched back to English. "You really are juéjiàng."

Jonas opened the door. "He's what?"

Lian crossed to her husband. "Stubborn."

Jonas kissed her. "So I tell him all the time."

Bo reluctantly got to his feet. "I see phase one is done."

"Yes. The brass is happy because this makes us look good. I presented just enough evidence to the press to keep them happy, without going into great detail. I'm guessing our friends Biao and Feng are rubbing their hands together in glee right now. We'll leak that a hit has been ordered tomorrow."

"It will not have to be a leak. Feng has already ordered a hit." Lian wrapped her arms around her husband's waist.

"He certainly did not waste any time. How will you get Feng to believe me dead if those he hired do not take credit?" Bo sat back down, exhaustion taking over.

"We have ways." Jonas just smiled and said no more.

Bo nodded. "It is your move, Brother. Make it a good one."

"I plan to."

Chapter Ten

Maryanne's labor had been a long one, but after sixteen hours, little Bryan had made his way into the world. Maryanne had given the baby her maiden name instead of her married name. With any luck, nothing of his father would taint his life, not even his name, though he would only have his birth name for a short while. And though Bryan's hair was dark and his skin darker than Maryanne's, Emma could see more of his mother's features in his tiny face than those of Ping.

Emma took a seat in the small waiting room. FBI agents were both inside and outside the building. Even Agent Cole had shown up, which had surprised her. Both he and his wife Lian were in the small waiting room. Not surprisingly, Agent Tanner had remained, and still remained, at Maryanne's side.

"You must be relieved." Lian took a seat across from Emma.

"Very. The baby came out a little over eight pounds, and the doctor assured Maryanne that all went well. They are both resting now. Maryanne is just grateful she didn't need a c-section." Emma rubbed her tired, blurry eyes. She'd spent most of the day with Fan, who had been with her mother until just shy of the actual birth. Fan was now sleeping on a foldout bed in Maryanne's room and Bryan in a small crib beside Maryanne's bed.

Jonas came to stand beside his wife. "I can have an agent take you back to the house so you can rest."

Emma thought about it. "Maybe in an hour or so. I'd like to check on Maryanne and the baby one more time."

One of the other agents went to the small television in the room and turned up the volume of a news story. Emma, though not interested in the television, turned her head at the noise.

The FBI agent turned to Agent Cole. "You should see this."

Emma watched, her eyes transfixed on the screen at the first mention of Bo Lee. The news reporter was outside a large courthouse where Bo was being taken for arraignment. She was hardly aware of getting to her feet and coming to stand before the television. She knew Bo had been arrested. Agent Tanner had told her and Maryanne. Maryanne had been relieved that at least one person was behind bars who might seek to harm her. All Emma felt was a sort of numbness.

Emma's knees buckled when a loud noise rent the air on the television screen and other people began screaming and running. Now transfixed, she watched as Bo took two shots straight to the heart and his body fell where he stood. The cameraman got a very bloody close-up before being shoved out of the way.

Emma heard the unearthly sounds but didn't realize they were coming from her. She felt arms come around her from behind, but it all seemed to be happening in a haze.

Her chest constricted, and she doubled over. She could hear a voice in her ear telling her to take deep breaths, but she couldn't obey. Her eyes were glued to the television as FBI agents tried to block the news cameras and other bystanders while they tended to the man on the ground.

Then the sounds around her became a loud buzz, and she couldn't seem to focus anymore. She could hear herself trying to speak, but the lack of oxygen prevented her words from forming. She felt herself being picked up and set down on the low sofa on the opposite side of the room. She saw Lian's face above hers, felt her hand holding hers. Finally, Emma's lungs took in a large gulp of air. And when they did, she felt hot tears burning her cheeks. She rolled over, away from Lian's kind gaze, and gave in to the unwanted grief as it took over her entire being.

Emma wasn't sure how long she lay like that. Once the storm of weeping subsided, she could hear Lian's voice speaking softly to her while the woman's other hand rubbed her back.

"Do you think you can sit up?" Lian pressed a cold cloth against Emma's forehead and wiped her cheeks.

Emma turned and let Lian help her sit up. She glanced at the television, but mercifully it was off. She turned questioning eyes to Agent Cole.

"My men have informed me that Bo Lee is dead. The investigation is underway. We'll find out who did this." Jonas came and took Emma's hand.

Emma didn't see scorn or disgust in Agent Cole's eyes, as she thought she would see. Her voice was hoarse when she spoke. "Why bother? You and I both know what he is."

Jonas handed her a bottle of water he had set nearby while Emma had wept. "I wanted justice, not death."

Emma took a drink, then another when her stomach didn't revolt. "Isn't death a kind of justice?"

Jonas handed her the bottle cap. "Sometimes. I know this can't be easy for you. And I do understand. Bo was my brother."

Emma's head snapped up. "What?"

Jonas took a step back and let Lian tend to Emma. "Not many people know. Knowing what he is doesn't make him less my brother. Sometimes it's hard to reconcile the man I knew with the things he had done. I have no doubt you've been struggling with it as well. Time will heal your broken heart, Emma, I promise."

Emma leaned her head on Lian's shoulder when the other woman wrapped her arm around her waist. She needed comfort and was willing to take it in the form of Lian's understanding. "I've been having a hard time believing what I have been told about him. And yet I can't doubt what I know. And I can't help but wonder if what I've been feeling is what Maryanne felt when she learned what her husband was. I don't know what to think, knowing Bo's dead. It seems so unreal."

Lian gave her husband an angry look over Emma's head. Jonas just shook his head.

Emma, unaware of the exchange, felt a renewal of tears but did her best to stem them. "I think I'm ready to go back to the house now."

Lian helped Emma clean up in the bathroom so she could see her cousin again before heading to the safe house.

Emma was grateful when the other woman remained with her while she said her good nights to Maryanne, Fan, and little Bryan. She took a moment to kiss her new cousin before allowing Lian to pass her off to one of the agents.

Lian watched as Emma left. Once out of earshot, she turned to her husband. "I certainly hope you know what you're doing. Do you think it wise to tell Emma that Bo is your brother?"

Jonas held Lian when she came and rested her head on his chest. "It seemed like the right thing to do. Thank you for being here. This wasn't quite how I wanted her to hear the news, but it had to be done."

Lian relaxed a little more against him. "Next time, tell your agents to keep the television off. But perhaps the shock of seeing it herself instead of you just telling her will make it more real."

Jonas tucked Lian against his side and headed out of the hospital. There were plenty of agents spending the rest of the night in the hospital, and he had plenty of agents outside the safe house. "The next steps will be feeding to the press that a rival organization here in the U.S. is responsible for Bo's murder. It will come across the news that the hit was a retaliation. Feng and Biao won't take it at face value right away, but once the right information is fed to the right people, they'll have no choice but to believe our version of the event. And with any luck, both men will be out of my hair and in the custody of the Hong Kong police before the month is out."

"Agent Cole." Agent Tanner trotted down the hallway, catching up with his boss before he left.

"What is it? Are Maryanne and the baby okay?" Jonas stopped just outside the lobby doors.

"Yes, they are both fine. Both asleep again. I didn't want to tell you over the phone or over email. What I need to tell you is a bit of a touchy subject."

"What is it?"

Tanner paused. "Is it true Bo Lee is dead?"

Jonas nodded. "Yes. It looks like an assassination. I've got agents working on it now. Why?"

Tanner looked around to make sure no one else was around to hear him. "Because now we don't have to worry about him finding out that he's going to be a father."

The news hit both Jonas and Lian like a ton of bricks.

* * *

It only took a couple of days for the FBI to announce that they believed an organized crime syndicate in the U.S. was responsible for the murder of triad leader Bo Lee on U.S. soil. Reports both inside and outside the FBI claimed that the organization responsible wanted Bo dead. They did not want outsiders, or any foreigners, staking a claim on their turf. Jonas shook his head. It read like a bad crime drama, but it played well in the press and had a thread of authenticity.

There had been a lot of buzz on the wiretaps, and Lian had been busy trying to see if anything was being spread about Biao's whereabouts or Feng's. There was chatter, most of it coldly thrilled among the various groups who wanted Bo dead. Some were angry they didn't take the shot, but most were gloating at his death. There were also a few celebrations happening by local factions, and Jonas was gathering as much intel as he could. Bo's death had stirred up a hornet's nest, and several groups were taking risks that they normally wouldn't take, thinking that the FBI was too busy investigating Bo's death to worry about what they were doing.

Jonas had not expected this outcome, but he was more than willing to capitalize on it. Within a couple of days, some of those men would be arrested. He was just waiting for a warrant to be issued and for the rest of the evidence to be collected. A task force was already being assembled to take the men down. With any luck, those men would lead him to the two he was looking for.

Maryanne and her small family had been moved. Agent Tanner insisted on staying on duty, and Jonas let him. It hadn't gotten past his notice that Tanner was a little too close to Maryanne for his liking but wasn't prepared to make a case out of it. Maryanne trusted Tanner, and that was enough for now. Jonas trusted that Tanner would do his job and protect Maryanne, with his life if it came to it.

Jonas snagged his gun from his desk and headed out. He saw Lian. He nodded at her, and she grabbed her coat.

"Is he driving you crazy yet?" Lian waited until they were in Jonas's car before speaking.

"Surprisingly, he's been very cooperative. And very quiet."

Lian thought about that for a second and supposed it made sense. "Facing the reality of your own death, even a fake one, must make one think about one's future."

Jonas flicked on his turn signal and got on the highway. "I think part of his problem is that he's never believed he had a future to worry about. He never thought beyond dismantling his father's empire. And in that, he has succeeded. The government has seized all his personal belongings and his home, but much to their surprise, Bo had a plan in place for the company. His business holdings are now under the control of several members of his board. The main holder being his legal number one that he's been grooming for the past few years. The transition is going smoothly, and the government isn't trying to interfere."

Lian watched the scenery fly by. "His holdings are a big part of the local economy. It's in their best interests to let it flourish, if possible. But I think I understand what you mean about him not thinking of having a future. Since we met him, he's had no fear of death. In some ways, I think he courted it."

Jonas continued heading north. "I think he's more afraid of the future and not able to grasp the fact that he has one. Bo Lee, the triad leader, might be gone, but Bo is not. It will take some time, but once things have cooled down, he will be able to come out of hiding under a new identity. I think he's more afraid of that than anything else."

Lian could understand. When she lost her parents, it was as if her identity had been taken away with them. She had floundered in the U.S. while living with her uncle. She had not been sure who she was now that everything she had ever known had been taken from her. She had ended up in a strange country, surrounded by people she didn't think she had anything in common with. Coming to terms with the changes in her life had been one of the hardest aspects of losing her parents, second only to their loss. While Bo's situation was a little different, he was now in a strange country with no identity.

Jonas made sure no one was following them as he made his way through the suburbs north of the city. He pulled into the driveway of a small home and drove around the house, so his car was not visible from the street. The neighborhood was not a quiet one, which was intentional, but the less attention he brought to Bo, the better.

Jonas and Lian found Bo watching the news.

Bo did not glance up. "How long do you think it will take before I become old news?"

Jonas helped Lian out of her coat and then shrugged out of his. "It's been a slow news week. Give it a couple of days, and people will have forgotten all about you. You still need to keep yourself indoors."

"I am beginning to hate these walls, and it has only been a couple of days. Tell me you have some good news to share."

Lian grabbed the remote and turned the television off. "Maryanne had her baby. A healthy baby boy she named Bryan. Agent Tanner is in love."

Bo was relieved to hear that everything went well. The second comment had him confused. Agent Tanner had not struck him as the sentimental type on the few occasions they had met. "Agent Tanner is in love? Maybe being shot fried his brain."

Jonas laughed, more because Bo was picking up more and more American phrases. "Maybe. Either way, he definitely has had a bit of an attitude change these past months since the shooting. Maryanne is smitten, too, but fighting it. She has a hard road ahead of her."

Bo knew Jonas had the right of it, but he did not want to talk about it. Mostly he wanted to forget, but he knew that was not going to happen. He could not stop himself from asking. "And Emma is okay?"

Lian was the one that answered. "You could find out for yourself."

Bo turned his back on her and faced the window. "I wish you would leave it alone."

Lian took a step forward. "You're family. We hate to see you like this."

Bo turned back, his eyes narrowed. He felt the anger that had been building up inside him bubble up. "Like what? You do not know me. Neither of you do. You do not know what I have seen, what I have done. I destroy lives."

"Self-pity is not attractive on you, Brother." Jonas laid his hand on his wife's shoulder.

"You know nothing about me. I destroyed the life of the first woman I loved. I destroyed the life of my own mother. I destroyed the lives of the men who looked up to me."

Jonas dismissed the last part of his statement. "Those men were criminals. Nothing you said or did was going to change who and what they were."

"Bo, you were a boy." Lian couldn't bear to see the pain buried deep in the depths of Bo's eyes.

Bo touched her cheek lightly, a gesture he realized he was making more and more as he grew closer to his sister-in-law. He jerked his hand away. "I was never a boy. Or if I was, I do not remember. I was groomed from the cradle to take over an empire. And that is what I did."

Jonas wasn't going to dismiss what Bo had done, not the good or the bad, but in the end, he had helped topple a criminal empire. "You helped take that empire down. Your business is now in good hands, and out of the hands of those who would use it to destroy lives. That means something. You set the trap that will catch Biao and Feng. The world will be a better place with them locked up."

"Doing the wrong things for the right reason does not make it somehow not wrong. I lied, I stole, I hurt people. I even killed. And I did many of those things before I realized what I had become. My life changed, and I became a cop, but I cannot take those things back." Bo's eyes darkened with memories.

"What did change you?" Lian couldn't stop the words from coming out.

Bo laughed harshly from where he stood, back in the shadows of the room. "A woman. Seems fitting. What else has the power but a woman to change a man? But she did not change me in the way you are thinking. I always knew what she was."

"What was she?" Jonas kept his voice soft, trying to coax the words from his brother. He, too, could see his pain.

"She was a prostitute. Her name was Chingmy."

"You fell in love with a prostitute?" Lian was shocked.

"You say that with such disdain. If it makes you feel better, I did not pay her. And she was twenty-four to my eighteen. So it was legal, at least by American standards, though I did find out later that my father had paid her, so think of that what you will. Female companionship was not always so easy to come by unless payment was involved. Or coercion. I could not exactly date a girl from outside my world. I did neither with her."

"What happened to her? You said her name was Chingmy." Jonas pulled Lian back to his side, not trusting what the next words from his brother's mouth would be.

Bo saw the move, and he gave his brother a cynical smile. "So little trust, yet you claim to care. But no matter. My father had her killed. I was already plotting then to try to stop my father. Though I did not mind all he was involved in, I had my limits. Chingmy's murder pushed me past that barrier. I think my father thought her death would bring me closer to the fold. He could see my hesitation. Instead, I went to the cops that very day. My father had taken the only thing I cared about away from me."

"You didn't destroy her life. Your father did." Lian wrapped her arms around her husband.

"No? I think she would have viewed what happened to her in a different light. But how about my mother then? I knew what she was. I knew who she was to me. I knew what he did to her, what he still did to her from time to time, though he grew tired of her as she got older. I did nothing to stop it. I did nothing to free her. I could have, but I chose not to."

"Why?" Lian blurted it out.

"Reasons? I suppose I had them, though they do not make my actions any more palatable. She was a pawn. She was not going to take my father down. No one would have cared. Had I freed her, any chance of taking my father down would have been ruined. I could not let Howard suspect I was working against him. She had to stay. But I made that choice, and she continued to suffer for it."

Before either could speak, Bo spoke again. "And you are wrong. Many of the young men who came to work for my father could have been saved, criminals or no. They looked up to me. Some were in awe, some just feared. Either way, I could have changed the outcome of some of those men's lives. Many died, and I let it happen time and again."

Lian left Jonas's embrace and went to Bo. He had once again turned his back to them. She wrapped her arms around him. "Bo, you are more than those things. Look at what you did for Fan and her mother. That counts for something. Emma misses you, even while thinking the worst of you."

Bo could not bring himself to step away from Lian. The pain in his chest was too great. But he could not think about Emma right now. "And what of Fan? I have hurt her as well, though she does not know it yet. I still have not told either of you the truth."

Jonas came and laid a firm hand on Bo's shoulder. "What truth?"

Bo took a deep breath and lightly removed Lian's arms from around his waist. He stepped into the faint sunlight coming through the windows. "Fan is not Biao's daughter. I did not know it at first. Her mother was a prostitute, one of many in my father's employ. When I dug into the records, I discovered the truth."

Lian remembered the picture of Fan. She could very well be Bo's. Anger began forming. "She's yours?"

Bo did not miss the anger in her tone. "So cynical. No, she is not mine. Chingmy was not the first prostitute I slept with, but she was the last. And I kept away from any female that might have ties to my father after her. I was going through my father's records shortly after Kang's death, seeing if I could find anything that would tell me where Biao might have gone to ground. I found Fan's original birth record. Howard is her father. He gave Fan's mother to Biao, and Biao believed he was the father. Biao has no idea the child is not his, or that the mother was spying on him and reporting back to Howard. I did not want anyone else to know he was not Fan's father because I feared what Biao might do should he find out. And honestly, I feared what he might do regardless, which is part of the reason I did my best to find her. He sells women and children, and Fan would fetch a good price. Maryanne, too."

That stopped Jonas in his tracks. The only thing he could focus on was that Howard was Fan's father. "We have a sister?"

Bo actually smiled. "We have a very lovely, very smart sister. And she is being well cared for. Maryanne adores that child and would protect her with her life."

"Does Maryanne know?" Jonas couldn't think of anything else to say. He had a sister.

"No. I have not told anyone, and neither will you. I will not have anyone challenging the adoption. Maryanne is Fan's mother. I will not have them separated."

"But what if Biao finds out?" Lian couldn't help but worry.

"I will produce papers that deny his claim."

Jonas had no doubt he would and could. "I suppose it is a given that you have proof of her paternity. You may be able to pretend she isn't our sister, but I can't."

Bo nodded. "I know. You cannot ignore her any more than you seem to be able to ignore me. But trust me when I say she is happy, and I will not be the one to destroy that."

Jonas shook off the shock. "Yes, she is happy. And I suppose you have the right of it. But when this clears up, I will tell Maryanne. She has the right to know, and I have the right to be involved."

Bo took a deep breath. "You will do what you must."

Jonas looked at Lian, then back at Bo. "There is something I need to tell you. Perhaps we should speak in private."

Bo looked at Jonas, then Lian. "Keeping secrets from your wife?"

"It's not my secret. It's yours. She already knows. Lian and I agree that it will be easier if it's just you and me."

Bo dismissed that. "You may as well say what it is you want to say in front of your wife if she knows. Might as well have it all out now."

"This is a very personal matter, but have it your way. I don't like keeping this secret. And if my wife has taught me nothing else, sometimes the truth is more painful than lies, and it's best to keep things to yourself until you feel the time is right. Given what you just said, I think it's time for the truth. All of it."

Bo nodded. "What is this secret?"

"Agent Tanner told me something Emma has told no one else yet. She's pregnant, Bo."

Bo fell back against the wall. Pregnant? "No."

Jonas heard the harsh, flat tone of Bo's voice and recognized that Bo was in shock. After what his brother had told him, Jonas knew this was not good news.

Lian looked at Bo. "Bo?"

Bo shook his head and left the room. He needed to get out. Disregarding his brother's orders to remain indoors, Bo yanked open the front door and ran off down the street. He disappeared into the crowd and did not stop until he came to the river path. He stopped and looked down into the depths of the water while fellow pedestrians walked past him.

Pregnant. He did not doubt his brother's words. Nor did he doubt he was the father. Emma was not that kind of woman. She would not have hopped from his bed to that of another man so soon after they had parted. He knew what kind of woman she was when he had taken her; he hated himself for wanting so badly what he knew he should not touch, but he took what she had offered anyway. He knew the consequences of getting involved with him. And now he had irrevocably changed her life, tying her to a man like him. A man with no honor. A man who was now dead.

Chapter Eleven

"Are you sure she wants to go through with this?" Jonas sat across from Emma, who was curled up on the sofa at the new safe house in Virginia. They had been moved a week after Maryanne had given birth.

Emma had sat beside Maryanne when Maryanne told Agent Cole she wanted to do anything she could to help him catch Ping. "Yes. Having two children looking to her for safety has hardened her resolve. She wants to do whatever it is that needs to be done to see Ping arrested and behind bars. She won't feel safe until he is."

Jonas sighed. Emma looked as if she hadn't slept much the past week. Her voice was hoarse, and she had dark purple bruises under her eyes. "All right. With careful planning, I think we can draw him out. With Bo gone, many of the local leaders have been feeling cocky. I think we can use that to our advantage."

Emma didn't even flinch this time at the mention of Bo's name. She wasn't sure when the coldness had descended, but it was a blessing. She only hoped that when her feelings thawed, she would find a way to cope. The baby inside her was making itself known to her more and more each day. She owed it to her child whatever protection she could.

It was with conviction that she spoke to Agent Cole. "I want to help in any way that I can."

Jonas glanced at the other agent in the room, and the man took the hint to leave. "I'll let you know. We'll need to separate Fan and Bryan from Maryanne for a short while. I may need your help with them. Fan will be more comfortable with you than with anyone else. But there is something else I want to discuss with you."

Emma's voice was wary when she spoke. "About what?"

"Agent Tanner told me about the baby, Emma."

Emma flinched and wrapped her arms around her slowly growing belly. "I asked him not to say anything."

"No, you asked him not to tell Maryanne, and he hasn't. But your child, Emma, is my niece or nephew. I want to help. Lian wants to help. Whether or not you're ready to accept it, you and that baby are now part of my family."

Emma curled up tighter. "You have a strange definition of family. If I were you, I don't know that I would want to accept Bo's child into it."

Jonas came and sat beside her on the sofa. "I do have a loose definition of family. Being adopted does that for some children. I have wonderful adoptive parents and siblings. And thanks to Lian, I have my birth mother back in my life. Whatever Bo was or wasn't, he was my brother. Not everyone is all bad or all good, Emma. If Bo had been given different opportunities growing up, I like to think he would have been a different man."

Emma smacked Jonas's hand away when he would have laid it over hers. "How can you say that? He kidnapped women and children and sold them like they were cattle. If he were alive, what do you think he would do if he knew I was carrying his baby? All the scenarios that come to my mind do not play out well for me or the baby."

"Why don't we take a drive, Emma?" Jonas left the room to speak to Tanner, who was outside Maryanne's door, then came back.

Struck by the odd request, Emma didn't fight him when he bundled her up in her coat and led her to his SUV. She buckled up and sat quietly in the confines of the car.

"I didn't want to say anything at the house, and I don't want us to be overheard. My superiors would be furious with me if they knew I was telling you this, though I think my wife would applaud me. I need you to swear to me you won't repeat what I'm going to tell you."

Numbly, Emma nodded. "I swear."

Jonas pulled into the parking lot of a fast-food restaurant and parked away from the building. He left the vehicle on but unbuckled his seat belt. "Bo was not all that you've been told. While I can't deny that he did many of the things he's been accused of, it's only half the story. If you were not carrying his baby, I would not have said anything. But as the mother of his child, you have the right to know."

Emma wasn't so sure she wanted to hear what Agent Cole was going to say, but she found herself nodding again.

"Bo was an undercover cop with the Hong Kong police department. He used his position as Alexander Howard's son to help take down a criminal empire."

Emma found her voice through the shock of Agent Cole's words. "I don't know who Alexander Howard is."

Jonas started from the beginning. "Alexander Howard was an American businessman who started a large export business out of Hong Kong. Somewhere along the way, he developed strong ties to a large triad. And though not Chinese, he ended up becoming one of the heads of it. He kept a woman named Naiwen Lee, whom he had bought when she was sixteen, and had two sons. First me, then Bo. Naiwen sent me to America to escape Howard. In retaliation, she was forced to have Bo, who was then taken away from her at birth. As Bo grew up, Howard groomed him to take over his empire. But Bo wasn't sold on all his father was doing. And though Bo never elaborated with me, I can tell you he was not okay with the selling of people. Guns, drugs, yes. People, no. Then one day his father did something Bo could not forgive. Bo went to the police. The police, in turn, used Bo to try to take Howard down."

"Tried to take him down?" Emma's heart was racing, and her head was pounding, but she was listening to every word.

"It's a bit of a long story, but Naiwen killed Howard when Howard attacked Lian. Lian was working undercover, and when Howard realized Lian had overheard a sensitive conversation, he took her captive. Naiwen couldn't take watching Howard hurt another innocent person, so she bashed him in the head with a statue. I met Lian when she located me in the U.S. as a favor to Naiwen, who wanted to know what had happened to her first son."

Emma smiled a little at that. It was obvious to anyone who spent time around Agent Cole and Lian that Lian adored her husband. And that Agent Cole truly loved his wife. "At least part of the tale has a happy ending."

"That it does. But to finish, Bo kept his activities quiet after his father's death. He used the time to legalize his father's business so that all the people in his employ would still have jobs should something happen to him. He used his inside knowledge to undo what the other leaders in the triad were doing. Even now, the police in Hong Kong are waiting for Biao to show. And they are actively seeking Bo's number one. Once both men are in custody, the rest of the organization that Howard led will break apart. Some will try to rebuild, but whatever the result, the power that Howard wielded all those years ago will be dismantled."

"Then why did you arrest Bo? He might still be alive." Emma's voice cracked as her tears built.

"As far as the world is concerned, Bo was a criminal. His activities within the sanction of the police and the government were well hidden. At this point, we could not risk anyone finding out he was not exactly what people believed him to be. And chatter came across the wires that his number one, a man named Feng, was hunting him, hoping to seize Bo's power. Bo and I felt it best if he were in the custody of the FBI."

Emma rubbed her wet cheeks. "So Feng succeeded."

"It was not his hand that took Bo's life, but ultimately, yes, his plan succeeded. It is the hope of the FBI that either we apprehend him, or that the Hong Kong police do so when he arrives back home. My superiors are of the opinion that they would rather let the Hong Kong police have him."

"What of Ping? Why try to trap him if you think he'll

go home too?"

"I have been tracking him for a while now. He knows too much about me and my family. He also knows Bo was my brother. I'd just as soon have him rotting away here in a U.S. prison as at home. And I'll be honest, I want the pleasure of taking him down, as well as the rest of his men. Bo wanted the police in Hong Kong to apprehend both, but I'd rather see to Biao personally."

Emma was quiet, taking in all that he had told her. She straightened in her seat. "Thank you, Agent Cole, for the truth."

"Jonas. Like I said, we're family now."

Emma closed her eyes and wiped away the last of her tears.

"First thing tomorrow, I'll have one of the female agents make you an appointment. You need to be seen by a doctor. You need to take care of yourself. The next few weeks are going to be hard on both you and Maryanne. Now how about we get some lunch?"

Emma opened her eyes and looked at the building they were parked outside of. For the first time in days, she was sure she could eat. She let Jonas take her inside.

Emma took a large bite out of her sandwich and was content to remain silent while they ate. After they were settled back into the SUV, Emma turned her attention back to Jonas. "I'd like to meet your mother. When this is all over, I'd like her to know her grandchild."

Jonas took Emma's hand. "I know she would love that. Lian and I have not been married long, and she is already asking us when we plan to have a child."

Emma placed her other hand over her stomach. "No matter how hard or painful it is, or no matter how sweet and fulfilling, life goes on."

Jonas squeezed Emma's hand. "That it does."

* * *

"Have you lost your mind?" Bo paced the small living room.

"I take it that's a rhetorical question." Jonas crossed his ankles from his prone position on the couch and let Bo pace.

"I told you to let the Hong Kong police take care of Biao." Bo wanted nothing more than to unleash his anger, but he kept it under a tight rein.

"And I'd rather know without question that Biao is no longer a threat. Maryanne wants him caught; she is willing to help, and I'm willing to use her to do what needs to be done. The plan is already in motion."

Bo growled and spun on his heel. "The whole point of my death was to get Biao and Feng out of the U.S."

"No. The point of your death was keeping you alive. You chose to believe what you would. But my plan has always been to keep you alive. I told you before, Brother, I do not want to see you killed."

Bo stopped his pacing. "I do not understand you. I do not understand why you care."

"The feeling is mutual. I don't understand you. You have spent the last few years of your life devoting yourself to taking down your father's organization. You have succeeded. Did you never wonder what life could be like after you completed your mission?"

Bo dropped onto a chair. "I never believed I would survive it. The mission always felt like a one-way trip. I have yet to decide if I should be thanking you or cursing you."

"If you weren't such a stubborn ass, you'd see what could be ahead of you. I won't keep harping on it, but I think it would be something to see your children and mine growing up side by side."

Emma and the baby. They were never far from Bo's mind. Emma's sweet face haunted his dreams. "You have yet to deliver a child, Jonas."

Jonas slapped his brother on the back. "But it is in my future. The future I am building with Lian. I know life has not been easy for you. It was not always so easy for me. I don't live with the same scars as you do, so maybe it's easier for me to embrace the future I see ahead of me. But trust me when I say your future is worth fighting for."

Bo was not sure what to do or what to say. Perhaps Jonas was right. Perhaps his future was worth fighting for, now that he had one. "Find Biao. Make sure Feng gets on a plane. While you are doing that, I will think about what you have said."

Jonas rose and grabbed his coat. "Good. Now I don't have to sick Lian on you to talk some sense into you."

Bo smiled at the thought of Lian being unleashed on him. "Your wife is very fierce."

"And loyal. She is willing to fight for those she loves. And despite your best efforts, she does love you."

Bo conceded. "And I her. And you."

Jonas stopped in his tracks and turned to his brother. He could see the moisture in Bo's eyes. He felt his own eyes sting. "And I you."

Bo turned away and went back to the window to look out at the uninspiring view and chose, for the first time in his life, to think beyond his mission. He thought of Naiwen and the freedom she finally found. He thought of his brother and sister-in-law and of the children they would have one day. But mostly he thought of Emma and their child. Bo knew he needed to decide what the best option for Emma would be. Was it him in her life? Or was it him as far away from her as it was possible to be? Once he decided the answer, it would determine which path his future would take.

Bo went into the bedroom and pulled out the laptop he had hidden there. Jonas would be furious with him if he knew he not only had the laptop but was using it. News reports only told him so much. He also needed the laptop to communicate with some old friends. Jonas had been right when he had guessed that he had been the one feeding information to the CIA. Bo's superiors had been blissfully unaware. But having the CIA trailing him gave legitimacy to his organization. The Hong Kong police had pretended to be unaware of what was going on under their noses in hopes of catching those working for him and those above Bo's position.

It did not take long for answers to his inquiries to come through. As of yet, Feng was still in the U.S., but that did not surprise Bo. Feng did not get where he was by believing what he was told. Even now, Feng would be trying to verify his death through his own methods. That is where Jonas feeding information to the right people would come into play.

But what was bothering him the most right now was Biao. Bo could see the trail Jonas was laying to catch him. A couple of hours later, his source said Biao had surfaced and was now in Virginia. Bo's gut clenched. Emma was in Virginia with her cousin. It was not a coincidence. Knowing he had no other option, Bo grabbed his cell phone, the one Jonas thought Bo had turned over to the FBI, and dialed his brother.

Jonas picked up on the second ring. "I swear, Bo, I am going to tie you up and search that house from top to bottom. When did you get your phone back?"

Bo ignored him. "Get your men over to the safe house. Biao is in Virginia."

Jonas sat up straight behind his desk. That intel had not come across his desk. "And how do you know that?"

"A mole."

Jonas gritted his teeth. "A mole, where?"

Bo went back to his laptop and sent Jonas what information he had. "I was not the only undercover cop on the case. A friend of mine who infiltrated Biao's gang a year ago has been keeping me informed of what has been going on in Hong Kong. Biao has been in touch with some of his men back home, ones who do not believe he betrayed his men. He is in Virginia, and he knows where Maryanne is."

Jonas would have cursed but figured it would be a waste of breath. He began shouting orders from his office.

* * *

Emma climbed out of the SUV and headed toward the safe house. Agent Ardell had taken her to see a local physician. Emma was glad to know she and her baby were healthy, though the doctor was a little concerned about how thin she was. The doctor gave her a script for some heavy-duty vitamins and told her she needed to start eating better. Emma had promised to start taking better care of herself.

Emma heard the agent answer her ringing cell phone as she made her way toward the steps. The doctor had also told her she needed to get some rest. Emma wasn't sure she'd slept a night through in weeks, not since the last night she'd spent in her own bed. Of course, her last night at home had been spent in Bo's bed. Had she spent that last night in her own bed, she wouldn't have found herself in this situation.

Emma was at the front door when she heard a loud shout behind her. She saw Agent Ardell coming toward her with her weapon drawn. A loud cracking sound had her dropping to the floor of the porch. Agent Tanner had been preparing both her and Maryanne on what to do should anyone find them. Emma saw Agent Ardell diving for cover behind the SUV. Emma realized the loud sound was that of a gun. The glass from the front window had been shot out, and Emma realized she was now lying on a pile of shards. She scooted on her belly away from the doorway. She stopped when she saw Agent Ardell motioning her to be still.

Emma did as she was told, but it did no good. Whoever was at the window had seen her movements. She heard shouting from inside the house, but the words weren't in English. Emma felt the back of her shirt being grabbed, and she was yanked to her feet. She could feel the breath of the man holding her against her neck. She could also feel the barrel of his gun pressed into her ribs.

"Hello, cousin. One down, one to go."

Emma realized it was Ping who was behind her. As he shoved her through the door, she could see two other men. Both were Chinese, and both were holding a gun. She trembled in Ping's grasp.

"Where is my wife?" Ping shoved her to her knees next to the sofa.

Emma shook her head. She didn't know where Maryanne was, but at least she wasn't here. Agent Ardell would keep them from walking into the same trap she had just walked into. When Ping raised his fist to strike her, she cowered at his feet, but then he stalked away from her. One of the two men was talking, and Emma could only imagine what they were talking about. A second SUV had pulled up in front of the house, followed by a third. Through the strands of hair that hung in front of her face, she could see Agent Cole exiting one of the SUVs. She could hear voices but couldn't make out the words.

One of the men grabbed her by her hair and dragged her to her feet. He shouted orders at her, but he obviously didn't speak English. He tossed her into one of the bedrooms, her bedroom to be exact. She ran for the window when the door closed behind her, but the window wouldn't budge. The house was meant to keep intruders out, and that also meant keeping its occupants inside. All the windows at the rear of the house had locks on them, and there was no way out of the bedroom except back through the way she had come.

Chapter Twelve

"How many are in the house besides Emma?"

Agent Ardell glanced up at Agent Cole. "I saw the one who grabbed her, and I could see two more men inside the living room. They must have bypassed the alarm system."

Jonas didn't glance down at the agent. Maryanne, Fan, and Bryan had been moved to a secondary location. Jonas had a second place secured for this purpose. Biao had tracked them a little quicker than Jonas had anticipated. Thankfully Bo's "friend" in Hong Kong had gotten wind of the move. They would be looking at a lot more hostages if he hadn't had the warning.

Agent Tanner came around to the side of the SUV where Jonas stood. "Are you going to try to negotiate with him?"

Jonas shook his head. "His first demand will be his wife. His second one is likely a one-way ticket out of here. I can't do either of those things."

"What's the plan?" Tanner kept his hand at the ready over his weapon.

"The mobile unit is on its way, so we'll have eyes inside the house soon. The cameras inside the house are short wave, so they wouldn't be detected right away. Ardell saw three men in total. Biao is definitely one of them. We also ran the faces of the other two men Ardell took pictures of before they closed themselves inside the house through our facial recognition software. Those two men we've seen before in other surveillance videos, but no names."

Tanner snorted at that. "A scumbag is a scumbag. But they're outmanned, and they know it."

"This house isn't rigged to blow, at least not yet. Who knows what toys Biao brought with him, but he has to know this isn't going to end well for him."

Tanner nodded. Last year he had not been at the house that Ping had wired to blow, but he had heard the stories from his hospital bed from other agents. "That won't stop him from trying to bring down as many of us as possible with him. Hopefully, he won't notice the cameras."

Jonas was doubtful they would stay hidden. By now, Biao had to realize he'd fallen into a trap. And without the hostage he really wanted.

Jonas heard his phone buzz against his leg. Having a feeling he knew exactly who was on the other side, he still checked the caller ID before answering. Cursing, he answered. "I'm a little busy right now."

"Where is she?" Bo was listening to the police scanner and had not heard anything come across the wire. But he had a bad feeling, and he was not one to ignore his intuition.

Jonas considered lying but couldn't bring himself to do it. And he didn't have to ask which "she" he was asking about. "Biao has her. Just her. I have the others at a safe location. He's got her holed up in the safe house with two other men. We're working on getting eyes on them now. I need you to stay where you are; I can't risk you being seen."

"You cannot negotiate with him. He will fight until death."

Jonas rubbed his brow. "I know. We're going to do everything we can to get her safely out of that house. We're working to determine the best plan. Just don't do anything stupid."

"You know me better than that." Bo's voice came softly over the line.

Jonas heard the call drop and cursed. He figured he had less than half an hour before Bo showed up here. He knew his brother wasn't going to sit back and hide while Emma was in danger. Though Jonas could sympathize, he needed to keep his focus on Biao and the situation in front of him.

Jonas saw Tanner wave him over. The live feeds were all set up for him to view. Jonas waved over the rest of the team. "We'll need to keep an eye on the perimeter. Biao was careless to have only brought two men with him. He could have more on the way. It's getting dark fast, and it would be easier to take us by surprise. Emma is in the bedroom in the middle rear of the house. We need to try to get her out of the house. We need to have men ready at the front of the house to grab anyone who tries to get her out or to grab the men should they realize someone is inside."

"Sir. We may need to rethink that plan." Agent Tanner pointed to the screen.

Jonas cursed when he saw Biao unzip the black bag lying on the table. Biao had come prepared.

* * *

Emma wasn't sure how long she sat on the bed in the back room. Her fingers were bleeding from where she had tried to pry the window open. There was nothing in the room she could use to pry it open, nor was there anything in the room she could use as a weapon. Her knees and belly were also bleeding where the glass shards had scraped across her body as she'd tried to belly crawl her way off the porch. All the wounds were superficial, and they weren't what was bothering her.

What really bothered her was that Ping didn't seem at all interested in her, nor did the men who were with him. She supposed she should be grateful, but all it did was make her more nervous. Emma knew the FBI was not going to negotiate with him. The only thing Ping wanted was what they couldn't give him. Emma wasn't naive.

Emma jumped when the lights suddenly went out. She jumped to her feet and pressed her ear to the door. She could hear the men in the other room talking, probably cursing about the electricity. She supposed the had FBI cut the power. It was a lot darker outside than she realized, and the room was nothing but shadows.

Emma stepped away from the door and sat back on the edge of the bed. She couldn't understand what the men were saying anyway. She scooted back and hugged her legs to her chest and prayed she and her baby would survive the night.

* * *

Jonas felt a small object hit the back of his leg. He glanced at the shadows nearby. Then a shadow moved. Jonas drew his weapon and headed to the side of the vehicle where he had seen the shadow move.

"Where is she?" Bo's voice was soft as he spoke to his brother.

"I told you to stay where you were. If anyone sees you, then everything we've gone through was for nothing."

"Let me do this, Jonas." Bo stayed kneeling by the side of the SUV so as not to be seen.

"He has a bomb. One sound, one hint that anyone is in the house, Biao will blow it. You said yourself he's not afraid to die. You go in there, you try to take him out, you'll lose Emma for sure, along with your own life."

"I do not care about Biao. Let me get Emma out. I can do it without being heard."

"I must have lost my mind. I can't risk my men if that house explodes. You'll be going in alone. Biao hasn't tried to make contact, nor has he responded to our calls. He's waiting for something."

Bo had a feeling he knew what that something was. This could also be a trap to prove for certain if he was dead or alive. Biao was probably waiting to see if Bo Lee was going to make an appearance. It was also possible Feng was in the vicinity. But none of that mattered. The sooner he got Emma away from Biao, the better.

Jonas shook his head at the men who took notice of their boss talking to himself beside the SUV. Jonas left only long enough to get a bag. Inside were tools Bo would need to get the back window open. Jonas briefly went over the layout of the house and which window from the back would be the right one. He then gave Bo an earpiece. Jonas waited until Bo had it in before speaking. "If Biao makes a move, I want you in communication with us. That bomb is not a toy."

Bo nodded, pulled the bag over his shoulder, and put a black mask over his face. He heard Jonas talking to the other agents, rallying them. Large spotlights were at the ready, but Jonas had opted not to turn them on, instead choosing to leave the men in darkness inside the house. But with no electricity, that meant no sounds. No fridge, no television, nothing to muffle any noise he might make.

Bo kept to the shadows, making sure that none of Jonas's men saw him. As he crept around the side of the house, he could make out the men inside through the thin curtains. Bo guessed they were using their cell phones as lamps, but the light gave away their locations. Bo disregarded the men and made his way around the back. In order not to give the house away as a safe house, the windows were normal glass instead of barred, though Bo would bet they were heavy-duty and bullet-resistant.

Bo made his way to the window without being seen. He could hear Jonas in his earpiece letting him know there had been no movement inside the house. He dropped the bag lightly to the ground and grabbed the tools needed to open the window as quietly as possible. He first used the glass cutter so he could unlock the window from the outside. He had the pry bar at the ready to open the window. Jonas had told him the windows were not easily opened otherwise.

From inside the bedroom, Emma crouched on the bed. She could hear the men in the other room arguing. She was pretty sure she heard one of them say "FBI," but of course they would know she was a hostage inside. Her only question was whether they would try to save her or not? It was her cousin who was the valuable asset, not herself. But she couldn't imagine they would just leave her here. Emma then heard sounds coming from outside the window.

She shot up from the bed and opened the curtains and blinds. It was so dark in the house she couldn't see much. Then she realized there was a figure in black outside the window. She felt her heart start to pound with both panic and relief: panic that her captors might decide to come to her at that very moment, and relief that help had come.

Realizing the man outside the window was attempting to undo the latch, she closed it and reopened it so he would know it was unlocked from when she had tried to pry it open. She heard something jam under the wood, and the window rose ever so slowly. Once there was room, she grabbed the bottom of the sill, trying to help the man outside. She saw the black hood and felt a moment of panic but got herself quickly under control. She had to trust that the man outside was trying to save her, not grab her.

In the quiet of the house, her breathing sounded harsh, as did the sounds of the window still being pried open. She tried to hold her breath to see if she could hear the men in the other room. She couldn't hear over the sudden pealing of the telephone. The house came equipped with a landline, and it had been ringing on and off since she'd been taken captive. Thankful for its loud, jarring ringing, she helped the man outside get the window open enough for her to fit through. She grabbed a small bag she kept stashed under the bed and climbed onto the windowsill and swung her legs out.

The man didn't say a word to her but gestured for her to reach out to him so he could help her jump the short distance to freedom. She trusted herself to him and almost sobbed in relief when her feet hit the grass. When she would have thanked the man, she stopped suddenly, seeing the faint green/brown color of his eyes in the faint light from the neighbor's house. Frozen on the spot, unable to believe what she was seeing but knowing those eyes could belong to no one else, she opened her mouth to speak but was stopped when a gloved hand covered her mouth.

Still reeling at the revelation of who had saved her, she felt her body being turned and then shoved in the direction of the side of the house. Self-preservation took over, and she ran for the safety she knew she would find on the other side of the house. Believing Bo was behind her, she didn't turn around to see if he was following her.

An agent she didn't know caught her and pulled her to safety. It was then she realized she was alone. Desperately she looked around but didn't see a figure in head to toe black. She saw Agent Cole talking on a comm device, and she ran toward him. She clutched at his arm.

Jonas saw Emma struggling to find her words, and fearing she might say something she shouldn't, he pulled her against his chest so that anything she might say would be muffled. He urgently spoke into comm device. "Don't do anything stupid. Get over here now."

Jonas cursed into the device again when he saw no sign of his brother making his way back around the house. Bo could only hear him; he couldn't respond. Fearing his brother was about to do something really stupid, Jonas ordered his men to fall back. He pulled Emma with him.

Emma was trembling, but she obeyed and didn't argue when she was placed behind a blast shield. Her eyes struggled to see what was going on, and she heard agents shouting to one another. She thought she saw a figure in black running alongside the nearby SUVs when a blast rent the air.

Emma covered her ears and dropped to her knees at the deafening blast. She was only vaguely aware of other people nearby who had done the same. The house was ablaze, and the firefighters who had been standing by sprang into action.

"Are you all right?" Jonas knelt beside Emma. His hands checked her over to make sure nothing had blown over the blast shield, striking her. He was relieved when Emma nodded but concerned when she didn't speak. He glanced over at the SUVs, saw Bo, and gave him a slight nod. He then watched as Bo disappeared into the shadows.

Jonas helped Emma to her feet. "I need you to forget what you saw, at least for right now. Do you understand?"

Emma glanced over to where Agent Cole had been looking and nodded. She was scared; she was confused. But she also trusted the man holding onto her. He and Lian had been kind to her, so she simply nodded.

Jonas left her in the care of the other agents, ordering one of the nearby paramedics to tend to the cuts on Emma's knees.   He watched dispassionately as the firefighters worked to put the blaze out. It would be a while yet before his men could get inside that house. But one way or another, he wanted positive proof that Biao was dead. Somehow this time he didn't think the man had been so lucky.

Once the blaze was out, and the house deemed safe enough to enter, he had his team collect what they could of the bomb device that had blown up the house. A few other men went in and bagged the charred bodies. It would take dental records to identify the men, but the right number of bodies were removed. Satisfied for the moment, Jonas went and found Emma. She had been sitting quietly to the side for hours.

"How are you doing, Emma?"

Emma pulled the blanket one of the agents had given to her tighter around her body. "I'm okay. Agent Ardell let me talk to Maryanne and Fan. She said they had been taken to a new safe house."

Jonas took her to his SUV, helping her into the passenger seat. He started it up and turned up the heat. He closed the doors so no one would hear them. "We believe Biao is dead. I can't say that Maryanne is no longer in danger, but the threat to her isn't what it was. There are men who would want to hurt her and the children simply because she was his wife.   She'll remain in custody. Eventually, she'll get a new identity, and she and the kids can start to live a normal life."

Emma's hands drifted to her belly beneath the blanket. "And me?"

"I'll see that you get what you want, whatever that may be."

Tears burned Emma's eyes, but they didn't fall. "He's alive."

Though her voice was not much more than a faint whisper, Jonas heard her. "It's best if you believe he's dead, Emma. Deep in your heart. Biao might be dead, but Bo is no safer for it."

Emma turned eyes filled with turmoil to Jonas. "And what if he's what I want?"

Jonas brushed a tear from her cheek. "I can only imagine what you're feeling right now. But Bo Lee is dead. There is no bringing him back. But as for the father of your baby, if that's what you want, I'll do my best. Is that what you want, Emma?"

So many feelings, so many emotions, were coursing through her. She was so angry that Bo had put her through his death. So angry that she had believed the worst about him. And yet she was so relieved he was alive. But did she want him back? She didn't know the answer.

Understanding her ambiguous feelings, he helped her buckle her seat belt. "Let's get you back to your family. I know you talked to Maryanne, but she probably won't sleep a wink until she sees for herself that you're okay."

Emma was quiet for a while, and Jonas was content to let her be so. She had so much going through her mind, and it was hard to land on any one thought. But overall, despite her own turmoil, she was glad to know Biao was dead. Maryanne no longer had to worry about him finding her or finding Fan and Bryan.

"What are you thinking?" Jonas had been watching various emotions play across Emma's face.

"That Maryanne is free of Ping. That Fan and Bryan are safe."

Jonas turned off onto a county road that would take them to the safe house. He saw lights coming up behind him. Recognizing the vehicle and the driver, he gestured to the back window. "That will be Agent Tanner right behind us. I think he's feeling almost as relieved as you are."

Emma wasn't sure how long it would take Maryanne to be interested in men again, but she had a feeling Agent Tanner would be waiting in the wings when she was. "I think we'll continue to see a lot of him."

Jonas pulled into the driveway of a house that was set off the road and was difficult to see behind the shelter of several old trees. The front door opened, and Maryanne stood in the light of the doorway, her young son in her arms.

Emma fumbled with her seat belt until Jonas helped her. She leapt from the SUV, the bag she had pulled from under the bed clutched to her belly as she ran to the front door. Jonas watched as the two women embraced. He could see tears coming down the faces of both women. He wasn't surprised when Agent Tanner came to stand next to him.

"We don't always get this outcome."

No, Jonas knew too well this was not always the outcome. But when it was, it made all the difference. "Stay here with them. I don't anticipate any more problems, but I don't want them alone. I have something I need to take care of."

Used to his boss's vague explanations, he simply nodded and went to the two women.

Jonas climbed back into the SUV, calling Lian as he backed out of the driveway. He gave a brief rundown of what had taken place that night, warning her he would be home late. He smiled when she told him she loved him and not to worry about her. He hit the gas and turned on his sirens. He had one piece of business to take care of before he called it a night. And he was looking forward to it.

Chapter Thirteen

"Want to tell me what happened tonight? You could have been killed." Jonas slammed the front door and didn't bother with pleasantries.

Bo sat on the couch where he had been for the past couple of hours. He had been waiting patiently for Jonas to show. "You cannot kill a dead man."

Jonas made a fist and took a step toward his brother.

Bo got to his feet. "You can hit me if you want to, but it will not do you any good. You will just hurt yourself."

Jonas let his fist sink into his brother's stomach. When his brother let out a satisfactory grunt, he then shoved him back onto the couch. "I have questions and you're going to answer them. No evasions, Bo. I'm not in the mood."

Bo rubbed his stomach where Jonas's fist had landed. His brother had quite the punch. "Not bad. But your technique could use some work."

Jonas didn't want to be amused but couldn't quite help himself. "We all can't be black belts, or whatever it is that you are."

Bo just raised his eyebrows. "You are in a mood tonight, Brother. You should be thanking me."

Jonas dropped onto the couch next to him. "As an agent, not as your brother, I need to know what happened tonight."

Bo interrupted. "For your report."

Jonas ignored him. "As your brother, and not as an agent, I need to know what happened tonight."

Bo relented. "Emma was exactly where you said she would be. She helped me get the window open. When she looked into my eyes, she knew who I was. I cannot be who she thought I was when I met her; I cannot be who she needs me to be now. I figured the least I could do was make sure she never came to harm because of me. I sent her on her way, and she found her way to you. I followed long enough to be sure she was safe. Then I went back to the house. I climbed through the back window and used the tools in the bag to pick the bedroom lock."

"What did you do?" Jonas had a sick feeling in his stomach. "You didn't trigger that bomb, did you?"

Bo rubbed his forehead, the headache behind his eyes growing more intense. "No. I had a different plan. One that would keep you from having to arrest me for murder. While Biao and his men were arguing, I grabbed the bomb he had left on the table and took it back to the bedroom. I did tamper with it, but I was only able to delay its detonation. Among the many things I have learned over the past year were explosives and timing devices. When I saw the bomb, I knew I could not defuse it, but I was able to borrow some time."

Bo got up and poured him and his brother a shot of whiskey. He handed a glass to Jonas and continued his story. "The men were fighting. They were angry with Biao. He set them up to die. Biao's plan wasn't to take Emma or to even find Maryanne; he wanted you. He believed I was dead, and he boasted about it. He wanted one last shot at you. He knew if he went back to China, he was a dead man. He knew if Feng found him here in America, he was a dead man. He wanted to take credit for my death but had been denied. He wanted yours instead."

Jonas swore and tossed back his drink. "And you weren't going to let that happen."

"You have much to live for, Brother. And no, I was not. The two other men were easy. Besides explosives, I have been training. When I went up against Biao last year, we were evenly matched. This time, I had the advantage. He got in a few good hits, but he was not going to win. When I had him pinned, he laughed at me. He managed to get the trigger out of his pocket. He was more than a little surprised when the house did not immediately go up. One good blow and he was unconscious. I ran from the house with just enough time to avoid the fate he had in store for you."

"People could have been killed. We could have gone in and taken them out once we had Emma secured."

Bo gazed down into the whiskey still in his glass. "I knew your men had pulled back. I also knew the houses on either side of the safe house were empty. I had watched you long enough. The only ones in danger were Biao and his men. The world is a better place without them. You know it as well as I do. And I knew, if I did not make it out of the house, you would take care of Emma for me."

"Emma is at a new location with Maryanne and her children. They are safe. I told her it was best to believe you were dead. She won't tell anyone she saw you, not even her cousin. None of my men saw you, either. My hope is Feng will be satisfied that you and Biao are dead and get himself off U.S. soil."

"You are working on new identities for all of them?" Bo finally swallowed his drink, hoping it would ease some of his tension.

"I think it's best all around. I don't know if anyone else would care about Maryanne, but I'd rather err on the side of caution. Their family can start all over and hopefully find some peace."

Bo thought of Emma's home. After her disappearance, the bank took possession. All of her things were sold off with the house. And as Emma had known, the neighboring homestead had purchased her land. She had no home to go back to, and because of him, she had also lost all of her possessions. There was nothing he could do to make it up to her.

"Will you go see her?"

Bo shook his head, but more to clear his thoughts than to answer Jonas's question. "I am a man with no name. A man with no past. What could I offer her?"

Bo set a hand on his brother's shoulder and squeezed. "A future. Perhaps not with Bo Lee, but with a new man; a man whose past can't haunt him and one whose past can no longer hurt her. You owe it to her to give her a choice. And be prepared, Bo, because she is not entirely sure she wants to see you. She fell for you, then thought you betrayed her. Then when she thought you were a criminal, after your death I told her otherwise. And now she knows you're alive, and that ultimately you're the one responsible for all she's been through."

"And that is why I should stay away." Bo's voice was harsh in the quiet of the house.

Jonas dropped his hand. "What you owe her is an explanation. You owe her an apology. And if she decides she does want you, you owe her that as well. That is your baby, your responsibility. I may not know you as well as I might have had we grown up together, but I know you are a man of honor, even if it's a bit tarnished. And you owe yourself the chance to be happy. Did Emma, during the brief time you had with her, make you happy, Bo?"

Bo, who had not shed a tear since he was a little boy, felt his eyes sting and a solitary tear slip past his control. "I do not know if I know what happiness feels like. But if what I felt was happiness, then she is the only person who ever made me feel it."

The two men were quiet for a while before Jonas broke the silence. "Want to get drunk? I need to get home, but I can sit with you until you pass out."

Bo laughed. "That is quite the offer, but no. Go home. What will you tell your superiors?"

"The truth. They know what is going on. The final report will look very different from what I tell them, but honesty is the best way. The doctored report will end up in the files, should anyone come looking. With any luck, your pal Feng will go home. And then I can concentrate on the next bad guy."

"You must be very relieved. I imagine Lian is too."

"You take it for granted that I told her what happened

tonight."

Bo was the one to clap his brother on the shoulder this time. "No doubt it was the first moment you were alone."

Bo walked Jonas to the door. "Xiè xie nǐ."

"That one I know. And you're welcome. Get some rest. You look like crap."

Bo closed the door behind his brother and locked it. He had told Jonas the truth of what had happened in that house. But had he not been able to delay the bomb, he still would have let Biao set it off. He meant what he said; the world was a better place without Biao in it. He had no compunction about letting the man kill himself and the two other men with him. And if that meant Bo had to die with him, then so be it.

But once again, Bo found himself very much alive, and very unsure of what his next move should be. Life was not something he spent much time contemplating, nor a future. But what if *Siming*, the Master of Fate, had decided to be merciful to him? Could he have all the things he never dared dream he would have? Having a real family was foreign to him. Meeting his brother had changed him in ways he never would have thought. Caring about someone was also foreign to him. Jonas and Emma had changed that. Lian, too, in her somewhat forceful way, had changed that. And though he did not know what Emma was feeling, Jonas and Lian cared about him. In some ways, he felt he owed them his life. He just was not sure he should be thanking them for it.

Because the first glass of whiskey he drank did relax him, he poured himself another and drank it in one large swallow. Alcohol was another one of those things he kept away from. He needed his wits about him, needed to be always in control. Martial arts helped him with that. In a life that was not his, in a life controlled by his father, self-control and self-discipline had become the most important things in his life. With self-control came the ability to take all the women who fawned over him, his father who hated him, and the men who served him to be pushed to the back of his mind. He could thank his training for his sanity.

Bo went to the window after shutting off all the lights. He watched as a light rain started to fall. He could picture Jonas now curled up in bed with his wife. He could picture Maryanne with Fan and her new son clutched to her side as she got the first good night's sleep she had probably had in years. And Emma. What of her? Did she lie in bed watching the same rain, thinking of him? Or had she determined that the best thing for her and their child would be to turn her back on him and pretend he never existed?

Bo knew Emma held his future in her small hands. He just did not know what he wanted her to do with it.

Knowing no answer would come, he went and contemplated the whiskey bottle. Perhaps Jonas had the right of it. Perhaps drinking until he could sleep would not hurt just this once. Bo poured himself another drink, then another, and continued to watch the rain fall until his eyes closed and sleep finally came.

* * *

A light knock on the front door woke Bo. Groggy, with

his head pounding, he opened his gritty eyes. He glanced at the clock. It was almost ten. Bo sat up, seeing the almost-empty whiskey bottle across from him. He was not sure how many glasses he had poured, but his throbbing head told him it was more than he had ever drunk before.

Another knock sounded on the front door. Jonas would not knock, so it was not him. Neither would Lian. Almost fearful that it might be Emma, he padded slowly to the front door. He glanced through the peephole. Shocked, he stood numbly on the other side of the door. It was not Emma, but the woman on the other side was not a stranger to him.

Hands noticeably trembling, Bo opened the front door. The petite woman on the other side did not say a word to him. She had dark hair heavily streaked with gray. She wore a flowered dress that was Chinese in style, with satin edging that fitted over her slender body. Her gaze was dropped to the ground, her body slightly bent forward, but he did not need to see her eyes to know they were a deep brown. Bo moved to the side so she could enter. He saw a man with iron-gray hair inside an SUV parked in the driveway. This man he also knew, though they had never met, and he was surprised he had not accompanied the woman before him to the door. He supposed some things had to be faced alone. He closed the door behind him, still unable to believe his eyes.

It was his mother who spoke first, her words in Mandarin. "You must be wondering why I came."

Bo tried to swallow, but his throat was too dry. Unsure how to respond, he simply nodded. But because her gaze was still on the wall and her back was to him, she did not notice. Bo finally was able to swallow the lump in his throat. "Yes."

Naiwen found the courage to turn and look up into the eyes of her youngest son. "That might be the first thing you have ever said to me."

Bo took a step into the room, a knot in his stomach forming that had nothing to do with the whiskey. "I suppose it should have been something more profound."

His sarcasm fell flat as Naiwen took a seat and folded her hands in her lap. Bo took a chair opposite her, far enough away so as not to scare her. He saw his mother as meek, timid. He knew what his father had done to her over the years, less as the years passed, but still enough to remind her that she was his to do with as he pleased. As always, to see her, to remember what was done to her, was to feel shame and guilt.

"My husband, Griffith, did not want me to come here. Jonas did not want me to come here, either. But he called me last night to tell me the man he was hunting was dead. I was relieved that the danger to him and his wife had been stopped. He called because he did not want me to be afraid for him anymore, but also that he was coming over. I knew then that something else was going on."

Bo suddenly realized that Naiwen should not be here. To her, he was dead. "How did you know I was here?"

Naiwen once again briefly looked at her son, then dropped her gaze. "When Jonas and Lian arrived at my home, Lian told me. She believed it wrong for me to think you were dead. Jonas did not agree but relented, and they told me together late last night. My husband was surprised, but somehow, I was not. Deep down inside, I did not feel you were dead."

Bo did not know what to say to that. And what he did say was not the most tactful thing he could have come up with. "No, but I suppose you wish I had stayed dead."

Naiwen's eyes shot up, and a small fire lit inside them. "No mother wants her son dead."

Bo rose and turned his back on her. "I have no mother. You of all people should know that."

It took more strength, more courage, than Naiwen thought she had to cross over to her son. Her hand shook as she touched his arm. "I know that I failed you."

Bo turned and staggered back, unable to bear having her touch him. "Failed me?"

Naiwen dropped her hand and her gaze. "I could not do for you what I had done for Jonas. I could not save you from him."

Bo broke. His voice rose even as his throat tried to close. "There was nothing to save. I was his son. I was destined to be what I became. I am the one who failed you."

Naiwen once again found the courage to look at her youngest son. In most ways, he was the son who resembled her the most. Jonas had some of her coloring but had the look of his father. In some odd way, it was easier to see Jonas, even seeing his father in his face, than it was to look at the son who favored her. Bo had been taken from her. She had fought, but she had lost. And until her second son had saved the life of her first son, she had believed Bo to be everything that his father was. Looking at him now, seeing the pain she never thought to see on his face, she realized that some of her lived inside him.

Naiwen reached out to him. She held her hand out until he found the strength to clasp it. Eyes wet, voice trembling, she tried her best to find the right words. "I am your mother. I was supposed to protect you. You did not fail me. I believed that at one time, but I do not believe that now. Jonas told me all about you, all that you did for him, and all that you have done since. It pains me more than you know to live with the guilt of not finding the strength inside myself to find a way to save you. Even when I believed the worst, the guilt remained."

Bo looked at their joined hands. Her hands were so small, small like Emma's. He only had one question left. "Why did you come here?"

Naiwen released him and went back to sit. Her legs were trembling, partially from lingering fear he would reject her, and partially from relief that he had not yet. She had not known how Bo would receive her. And it was that fear that had kept her from coming to him sooner. But she did know he deserved an answer. "Mostly Lian. She told me about a woman named Emma. She said she is going to bear your child."

"Lian talks too much." The words were true, but he found he could smile.

Naiwen clasped her hands in her lap. "Lian thinks you love her. She also says you will not go to her. I think you deserve a second chance. I got mine."

Bo took a deep breath. He never believed in second chances before, but the part of his soul that was intact was starting to. "I did not want to want her. I did not want to feel responsible for her, or anyone else. But every moment I spent with her, every time I was near her, I ached for her. But no matter what I want, she deserves better."

To argue with him would have been a waste of breath. Naiwen did not know her second son, but she knew some of his father lived inside him, and perhaps that is what Bo was really scared of. "You were afraid you would hurt her."

It was not a question, and it was nothing but the truth. "Yes, I was afraid I would hurt her. She is not like other women I have known. And in the end, I did hurt her. Just as I knew I would."

Naiwen was not naïve. She knew the kind of women his father had around him and knew her son had the same. They were worldly women, women who were only looking out for themselves. Some had no choice, and for some, that was their choice.

Naiwen leaned forward. "Griffith, not long after I met him, told me that I had to leave the past in the past. He said I had much to offer the world if I would just embrace it. He told me to embrace the woman I always wanted to be and to shed the woman I was forced to become. That is what you have to do. You have to shed what was and embrace the man you can be, the man you want to be. Maybe your Emma can help you do that."

Bo heard the words, but it was more the tone that had him responding. "Sounds like something Jonas might have said to me. Why did you really come here today? Guilt?"

Naiwen nodded. "Partly. It was a big part of it, to be sure. But I think I am part of the reason you will not go to

Emma. I thought maybe I could change that. You deserve the truth, just as your Emma does. You were right, part of me was relieved when I heard you were dead. But not because I wished you gone, but because then I would not have to face you. It had taken me almost a year to get used to Jonas in my life. I feared what he would think of me. Feared that he would be angry with me for sending him away. And yet, I feared you more. Feared what you would think. Feared that you would not forgive me for not sparing you the legacy of your father. I feared you would hate me. I knew I could not bear to see hatred in your eyes, but I knew I could not avoid you forever."

Bo rubbed his eyes, his voice hoarse when he spoke. "I do not hate you. I could not hate you. I know what you lived through, what you endured. And sadly, for many years I did not care. And then Howard took the one thing I cared about, and my life changed forever. If anything, I hate myself, not you. I hate that it took so long for me to come to my senses. I hate knowing that given the same choices, I would make them again. After what he did, I wanted him dead, but I had a duty to see him arrested. I wanted him to pay for all he had done to so many people. That included you, but mostly my motives were selfish. The day you killed him, you freed me from him. The Hong Kong police would have arrested him; I would have arrested him, had you not killed him, but it would not have been the same. I thought I would find pleasure in his rotting away in prison, but in some ways, he still would have had a hold over me. So do not hate yourself. It took you longer, but you did save me from him."

Naiwen could not hold back her tears. She wanted to go to him, but neither of them was ready for that. But perhaps today they had made a small connection and taken a small step.

Naiwen wiped the tears from her cheeks. "What will you do now?"

Bo glanced at the clock. Only a short time had passed. "I need to talk to Jonas."

Naiwen nodded. "You will go to her?"

Bo gave her the only answer he could. "As soon as I figure out where she is."

Chapter Fourteen

It had taken a bit of groveling on his part to get Jonas to tell him where Emma was. Bo figured his brother was getting even for all the grief he had given him over the past months they had known each other, and more specifically grief over his taking so long to admit he needed to see Emma. And of course, once Jonas agreed to tell him where Emma was, it was only with the stipulation that Jonas take him.

So here he was sitting in the back seat of Jonas's SUV, with Jonas and Lian in the front seat. It also did not surprise Bo that Lian insisted on coming. Since he owed Lian a great deal for sending Naiwen to his safe house, he was not going to argue. And he supposed there was a part of him that did not want to face Emma alone. It had been months since he had truly seen and spoken to her. The last time her lips had been swollen from his, her body still flushed from their lovemaking. The vision of her naked, the light from within the cabin glowing on her skin, had tormented him since the day he lost her.

And heaven help him, she was pregnant with his child. The idea of a child had been surreal, almost unbelievable. He could not picture Emma pregnant, her breasts and belly swollen from his child growing inside her.

"We're here, Bo." Lian spoke softly from the front seat of the SUV.

Bo glanced up. The house had the same look as the one he had been staying in. Bo pulled the hood Jonas insisted he wear further over his face. It was not likely anyone would see him, but if they did, he and Jonas did not want anyone to be able to positively identify him.

The person at the front door was not Emma, but Tanner. He was holding Bryan. "Come on in. The women are resting. As you can imagine, they both had a rough night."

The trio entered the house, and Jonas closed and locked the front door. Tanner set the alarm. He went over to Fan. "Remember Agent Cole and Miss Lian?"

Fan nodded and pressed herself against Tanner's legs. She looked over at Bo and pointed her finger. "I remember him, too. He was at Auntie Emma's house."

"How are you, Fan?" Bo crossed to where his sister was gazing at him from next to Tanner.

"I got a new brother."

Bo looked over at the black-haired child Tanner was holding. "So I see."

"When Emma admitted you were alive, I was afraid you would show up." Maryanne spoke from a nearby doorway. She closed the door behind her; the animosity in her voice was unmistakable.

Bo gave her a slight bow. "I would like to see Emma."

Maryanne crossed and poked him in the chest with her index finger. "Haven't you done enough? She doesn't need you. She has her family. And you aren't it."

Bo held his temper in check. Maryanne had no reason to trust him or to like him. "I am going to try to change that."

Maryanne shoved him, her own temper fraying, and the stress of it all finally getting the best of her. "You lied to her. You got her pregnant. You disappeared. And you let her think you were dead. Worst of all, you let her think you were a criminal. And you know what. You are. You're no better than Biao."

Bo took the insults, as well as the verbal and physical jabs she was throwing at him. And he could not blame her. He should have been trying to help her, help her cousin. Instead, he had been there for his own selfish reasons, and those reasons had not been in anyone else's interest but his own.

Maryanne didn't take long to tire, and her hands dropped at her side. "After what you did, you at least owe Emma the truth."

A voice came from behind the group. "It's okay, Maryanne. I understand."

Bo heard Emma's voice, and there was nothing that could stop him from crossing to her. Her hair was a little longer, though still the same honey shade. He could see purple bruising under her eyes. Her cheeks were hollow, and her eyes were dulled. This was not the vibrant woman he remembered. It was as if a light had gone out inside her.

He could not prevent the sharp inhalation of breath when he took in the rest of her. Despite the weight he could see she had lost in her face, the rounding of her once flat belly brought home to him what he had done. And if he had any thought about whether she was happy to see him, happy to be having his child, that hope was dashed.

"Why are you here, Bo? Ping is dead. Shouldn't you be on a plane back home?"

"I needed to see you."

Maryanne came to stand beside her cousin. "Yeah right. You haven't had the urge to see her in the months since we've been in custody."

Emma put a hand on Maryanne's shoulder. "It's okay. I understand."

"So you said. Just what is it that you understand? That he's selfish? That he's a jerk? That he's no better than Ping?"

Emma stilled her cousin's tirade. She looked at the rest of the group watching them. Lian had her arms wrapped around her husband's waist. Tanner was trying to calm Fan, who didn't understand what was going on. She then looked into Bo's eyes. "We should talk alone."

Bo did not dare touch her. "Come with me?"

Emma stopped Maryanne before she started up again. "Yes."

Jonas unwrapped Lian's arms from around him and came to stand next to his brother. "Why don't you pack up a bag. You two need privacy, and the sooner I have Bo away from here, the better I will feel."

Emma shrugged but then glanced at the bag behind her in the bedroom that held nothing but a family portrait, a couple of pieces of jewelry, and a can of seeds. They would be safe with Maryanne. "I don't have anything to bring. What little we had was lost in the explosion."

Bo would have cursed but held his tongue. He had not thought of that. "There are things at my safe house you can use."

Emma hugged her cousin. "Don't worry. I'll be fine. You need to rest. And I need to talk to him without little ears."

Maryanne glanced over at her two children, both snuggled up against Tanner. Feeling tears forming again, she nodded. She crossed to them and took Bryan in her arms. Tanner picked up Fan.

Emma went over and kissed both Bryan and Fan on the cheek before following Jonas and Lian out of the house. She was very aware of Bo behind her. She opened the door and slid into the back seat. She was careful to keep her eyes off Bo, who sat across from her. There were so many feelings, so many emotions inside her, and she couldn't sort them out. She stayed quiet during the trip and tried not to think.

In short order, Emma found herself alone with Bo. He looked the same. She wasn't sure why she thought he would look different. Perhaps because he was not the man she had met months before. Because he wasn't the man she had been slowly falling in love with.

"Are you hungry?" Bo stood uncertainly in the middle of the living room. He had expected Emma to tear into him the way Maryanne had. Instead, she was calm and watchful.

"No." Emma kept her eyes on his.

"You want to take a bath or something?"

"No. I want answers."

Bo went and set the alarm system. It was identical to the one in the other house. "You deserve them."

Emma took a seat on the couch and tried to hug her knees to her chest. Her stomach made that difficult. "I don't know if it's a matter of deserve. I've earned them, perhaps. Jonas said you are responsible for Ping's death."

"He is responsible for his own death. I just helped him on his way."

Emma closed her eyes for a moment. "Maryanne is free of him. It feels odd to know she is free to do what she wants, to go where she wants. I'm grateful he can never hurt her again."

"Or anyone else."

They were both quiet. The ticking of a clock in the kitchen could be heard in the silence. Bo finally sat on the opposite end of the couch. "I do not know what to say."

"Say you're sorry." Emma came up on her knees.

"I am sorry, Emma."

She searched his gaze and came to her feet. She walked the short distance until she stood before him. With a sob, she came down beside him and burrowed into his chest.

Shaken, his arms came around her. He gathered her closer until she was in his lap. He could feel her tears soaking the front of his shirt. With his own eyes stinging, he buried his face in her hair, unable to believe she was in his arms. That she trusted him enough to turn to him.

Emma wound her arms around his neck and could feel her breasts and belly pressed against his hard chest. Just hearing the sound of his harsh breaths, hearing his heart beating fast against her ear, soothed her. The deep ache that had burrowed in her heart eased enough so that every breath wasn't a struggle.

"I am so sorry, Emma. I never wanted to hurt you like this." Bo closed his eyes and simply held her, absorbing the feel of her.

Emma eventually pushed against his chest and sat up so she could look at his face. She knew her face was red and splotchy from tears but didn't care. She pushed her loose hair back from her face and then got to her feet. She went back to the opposite side of the couch.

"I deserve an explanation. All of it. How did you end up as an undercover cop? Why did you come to me? Before, not now. What were you looking for? Just Ping?"

Bo rubbed his eyes and carefully chose his words. "I do not know what Jonas told you. We share parents, though we did not grow up together. He grew up here in America and eventually was adopted by the Coles. I grew up in Hong Kong, mostly, with my father."

Emma stopped him. "Jonas told me a bit about your father. He said that you became a cop so you could take him down, but he died a couple of years ago. Why did you not get out then? Jonas said you were tracking Ping when you came to the U.S."

"There was no way out. My father had no choice but to leave me his empire. I had a duty to the people who worked for him. And if I maintained my power and gained his, then I could help the department take down others in the organization. I could destroy my father's empire and make sure no one stepped in to pick up the pieces. Biao was a piece. He was not the most important piece, but Biao had something more important."

Emma wrapped her arms around her waist. "What?"

"Fan. She is not Biao's daughter. She is Howard's daughter."

It took a moment to absorb what he said. "Fan is your sister?"

"Yes. I did not tell Jonas right away, though he knows now. I needed to know she was safe from Biao. Jonas will find it hard to stay away from her once he tells Maryanne."

Emma realized the impact, and her voice rose. "But what about Maryanne? You can't take Fan from her."

Bo came close enough to take her hand. "Neither Jonas nor I want to take her from Maryanne. No one else has to know. Legally Biao was her father, and the adoption is legal. No one will dispute it."

Emma relaxed. "This is so confusing."

Pressing his luck, Bo pulled her against him again. He let out the breath he had been holding when she did not pull away. "I never meant for what happened between us to happen. I knew I was lying to you. I knew you would be angry if you knew. And if anyone knew I was with you, you could have been in danger. But it seemed safe enough to stay for a while. I wanted to tell you. Any chance I might have had to do that ended when Jonas came in with the cavalry."

Emma closed her eyes and relaxed. "You did try to warn me, I suppose."

Bo tipped her chin up so he could look into her eyes. "I cannot undo what I did."

Emma simply laid her head back down. "Where have you been? Why did you fake your death?"

Bo knew he could not continue to keep any more

secrets. "I knew Biao would be looking for me. I was not worried about him. But Jonas came to me and told me that a man named Feng Wong was also hunting me. He works for me and wants what is mine. If he can find me and kill me, he can take my power and position. Back home, my men believe me dead, but Feng will want to be sure before he leaves."

"And when he leaves?" Emma had to believe this other threat would simply leave.

"He will be arrested if he returns. My superiors and I have laid a trap."

Emma heard what he was not saying. "You don't believe he'll simply leave."

Bo hesitated before nodding. "My death was very convincing. But it also was very convenient. While the right people have claimed responsibility for my death, and I have remained hidden while Jonas tries to track him, he will not take it at face value. He will be on the hunt for proof as we speak. Once he is convinced I'm dead, then he will leave. But not until then."

"Do you think he'll believe you had something to do with Biao's death? Were you seen?"

Bo ran his hands over her hair and rubbed her back. "You, Jonas, Lian, Naiwen, Maryanne, Fan, and Tanner are the only ones who know I am not dead."

Emma remembered Jonas's words. "Jonas said I had to believe in my heart that Bo Lee was dead."

"And Jonas will have gone back to Maryanne and your family to make sure they understand that, too. It was a risk to let them see me, but I owed you that much."

Emma pulled away. "You didn't feel that way last month, or the month before, or the month before that. Why now?"

"Naiwen. My mother." He stopped, realizing what he had said. He rarely admitted it aloud that she was his mother.

"Bo?"

"Sorry. I have been in the States for almost a year, but I could not face her."

"Why?"

Bo dropped his head and rested his hands on his knees. He told her about his father and what his father had done to his mother. He explained to her about growing up knowing who she was but ignoring her. He even told her that it was not until he was almost a man that he realized what his father was truly capable of.

Emma heard his words, and her heart ached for the little boy Bo had been. To have been raised by a monster, to know what the man was capable of doing to women and children, had to have been something that molded Bo, for good and for bad, into the man he was. "What made you open your eyes to what he was?"

"A woman." Bo did not want to finish the story, and he practically choked on those two words.

"Bo, please."

Bo took a deep breath and tried to center himself. "I fell in love. I knew what she was, but I thought that things would be different between us."

Emma realized she was going to have to pry the story from him. "What was she?"

Bo swallowed. "I believe the politically correct term here in America is prostitute. She worked for my father. She was older than I thought, though I knew she was older than me. But she acted as if there had been no others before me. We went to movies, we went to parks, we went out to eat. It was all so normal. I desperately wanted to be like all the young men I went to school with, and she gave me some of that."

Emma tried not to judge, but it was hard not to. "You fell in love with a prostitute?"

Bo heard the harsh tone. "It was easy to forget. And it was not as if that was what she dreamed of doing as a little girl. Her father sold her to mine. I guess some young, idealistic part of me thought I could save her. I thought that we could have a normal life, away from the dark world we both came from. Some days, the thought of being with her, living in a home in the country and raising a family one day, was all that kept me sane."

Emma placed a hand on Bo's arm. "You wanted to save her. It was a noble thing."

Bo placed a hand over hers. "In the end, she was going back to my father, telling him what I was doing. Howard felt I was getting too close to her. He could feel me pulling away from him, wanting something he had no intention of letting me have. He had his man, Feng, kill her."

Emma fought tears. "The man who is hunting you, the man who works for you? How did you…"

Bo placed a finger over her lips. "When she was killed, it became all too easy to stay behind, to start making new plans. It was easy to pretend to be what he wanted me to be when revenge lived in my heart. I dreamed of the day I would lock my father up, along with Feng and every other man who worked for him who hurt and exploited women and children."

Emma looked into Bo's eyes. "What was her name?"

"Chingmy."

Emma repeated the name to herself, trying to picture the woman Bo had loved. "Was she pretty?"

Bo felt a small smile tug at his lips. "Yes, she was pretty. She had long black hair, deep brown eyes, and the prettiest smile."

Struggling with an unexpected feeling of jealousy, Emma thought back to what he had said at the beginning. "You said you were young. Were there others?"

"Other women?"

Emma nodded.

"There were others, but they were not important. And they were never innocent. They never got close. But at some point, it got tiring. Before my father died, I tossed aside all other pursuits to focus on taking down the heads of my father's empire. That was my life's focus until I found out about Jonas, and then Fan. Then I came here to the States. I met Jonas. Circumstances dictated that I had to tell him I was a cop. By then, I did not particularly care about Biao. I knew Jonas would catch him eventually. But I started to become attached to Jonas and Lian, and I knew I owed Fan protection, if nothing else. That is how I ended up on your farm."

Emma brushed away fresh tears. "I'm guessing Jonas had something to do with faking your death. You strike me as a hands-on, one-step-in-front-of-the other type. I can't see you just faking your death and stepping aside."

Bo brushed away the last of her tears. "Jonas made me believe that I could have a life. That I could have a family, that I could have a future. He made me believe in hope. So I agreed to his plan. I thought being as far away from you was the best thing for you, so I stayed away. Then he told me about the child. And it only made me more resolved to stay away. Then my mother came. I want to tie my life to yours. To see what we can be."

Emma took one of his hands in hers. She placed it over her stomach. "I don't know what the future holds, but this child is life. This child is the future. I held onto the hope that Jonas would find Ping, and that Maryanne and I would be able to live out the rest of our lives with our children, seeing them grow."

Bo flexed his hand on her stomach, his eyes troubled as he touched the reality of his child inside Emma. "I was always so careful. I was not planning on anything beyond apprehending Feng and the others. I did not think I would survive it."

Emma realized that Bo wasn't really talking to her. His entire focus was on her belly. She rose, breaking the contact. "Maybe it's because I'm all cried out. Or maybe it's because I went through so many different emotions over the past months. Or maybe it's because I am just so tired. But, Bo, I want this baby. I am not sorry for it. I am a grown woman; I know how babies are made, and I know how to prevent one. Not once while we were together did I stop to think about it. I don't know what that says about me. Deep down, I knew you wouldn't stay, and I knew you didn't want me, not really."

Emma took a deep breath and continued. "And I know you are not as happy as I am about this baby. But this child is a reality. Whether you stay or go, or whether I decide I want you with me if you do stay, I will never wish this child away. You say you want to tie your life to mine, but I don't know if you really understand what that means. If you even know how to live the life you now claim to want. And I don't know if that life is really what you want. I think you feel you don't have a choice, that fate has made this decision for you, just as your childhood and who you would become as a young man were decided by your father."

It pained him that his feelings were so transparent. He could not help but feel both angry at himself for being so careless and in awe of the child she carried. And she was right. Part of him did feel his future had been decided the moment he took Emma in his arms against his better judgment. But Emma was not pushing him away, and she did not seem angry with him for feeling torn about the child. Overall, Bo supposed her lack of anger was better than he deserved, and now was not the time to try to figure their future out, or to force her to make a decision. But no matter what he felt, no matter what she thought, he did mean what he said. He wanted her life tied to his.

Instead of saying anything more, Bo stood so he could look down on her. "You should rest."

Emma could feel fatigue weighing on her. It had been almost twenty-four hours since she realized Bo was alive. In that time, she had slept little, though she had forced herself to eat. "I need something to sleep in. And where?"

Bo went to his bedroom and pulled out a black t-shirt for her to wear. He then grabbed a few necessities from the bathroom for her and led her to the other bedroom.

Fifteen minutes later, all ready for bed, Emma lay down under the covers. She could hear Bo in the living room. A little while later, she heard the other bedroom door close.

"So what do you think?" Emma placed a hand on her stomach. Then she sighed. "Yeah, that's what I was thinking too."

Emma tossed back the covers and crossed the hall. She opened Bo's door. "Bo?"

He sat up, and Emma could see his bare chest gleaming in the faint light. She felt her heart flutter a bit at the sight. She felt nervous coming to him, but the thought of lying alone all night, with the memories of being held at gunpoint and experiencing a bomb blast up close and personal, had her overcoming her nerves and entering the room.

"Do you need something?"

Emma closed the door behind her and climbed into bed with him. He was stiff beside her as if he were unsure of what to do with her in his bed. Emma tugged the blankets up to her neck, brought her pillow closer to Bo so she could place a hand on his chest. Sighing, her whole body relaxed; she breathed her words against his chest. "I don't want to be alone."

Bo watched as she dropped off to sleep, her arm draped over his chest. Turning on his side so he could pull her closer, he closed his eyes and savored the feeling of having Emma once again in his arms.

Chapter Fifteen

Bo did not say anything about Emma being pressed against him all night as they sat across from each other at the breakfast table. Emma looked rested, though she still had shadows under her eyes. He went about making them breakfast.

Emma declined coffee when he offered it but didn't hesitate to take the bowl of rice cereal from him and a small pile of scrambled eggs. When she finished her food, she leaned back in the chair and stared at Bo. It was hard to believe he was sitting across from her. "What are your plans, Bo?"

"In general, or today?"

"Let's start with today."

"First plan is to get you some new clothes. Jonas already messaged me that Agent Ardell will be by to get you."

Emma glanced down at the black t-shirt she was still wearing. "With Ping dead, it doesn't seem like we need protection anymore."

"For Maryanne, perhaps, though there is still some residual risk. But that baby inside you makes you a prime target."

Emma's head shot up. "No one knows about this baby,

and you're dead."

Bo took Emma's hand, thinking again how small it was. "As long as everyone believes that, you are safe, but if someone thinks I am alive, or if anyone digs and tries to find out where I have been, you will be a potential target."

Emma paled. "You mean Feng, don't you? But my home was sold. I used Agent Ardell's phone to see the sale online. If anyone comes looking for you, they won't find an owner who knows you. Do you think there is any danger to them?"

Bo shook his head and squeezed her hand. "No. The story would be easy enough to check out. But it will raise the question of what I was doing there. If I am lucky, everyone will believe I was simply waiting for Biao. What worries me is your boyfriend and his big mouth. If he were to mention a relationship between us, that would change things."

Emma hadn't thought about it, but Lonnie would most likely tell anyone who wanted to listen how she'd gotten cozy with the Chinese man, though he would use derogatory language. She turned her hand over in his. "Lonnie and I parted on bad terms. Told me I must be desperate if I had resorted to you. As you can imagine, he wasn't too thrilled to see me with another man. Even though he was the one to break it off, he always felt like he still owned me."

"Lonnie is the only risk. Regardless of who owns your home, I am not really worried about them. The sheriff there knows who I was and why I was there. And my having lived on your property waiting for Biao will not be earth-shattering news to the men who might come looking. Since there is no chance anyone would link me to you after you went into FBI custody, I think you will be safe. But I do not want to take chances. No matter what happened, no matter what might happen, I care about you, Emma."

It wasn't a declaration of love, but given what happened to him, she supposed the fact that he even cared about her at all was a step in the right direction. Some women might think she should throw that back in his face, reject him and his lukewarm feelings, but it wasn't in her. She went from thinking he was a criminal, to thinking he was dead, to knowing he was a cop, to finding out he was alive. In five short months, she'd run through every human emotion, and she was simply too tired, too tired to fight him, to toss his words back at him. What she wanted was him, him with her, him caring for her, and him being there for their child. Now was not the time for pride. Unless he didn't want her and the child.

Emma pulled her hand away. "What are your plans after today?"

"I always had a contingency plan. I figured if by some small act of fate, I survived the showdown while taking the organization down, I would need money and a new identity. The FBI, thanks to Jonas, is working on that new identity now. And I have transferred and hidden the money I had set aside. So right now, I am working on purchasing a home under that new identity. If you are willing, I want to take you with me. Maryanne and the children will get theirs, and you will get yours. But I want yours tied to mine. It will only take one call to Jonas."

Her life tied to his. She placed her hands over her belly, knowing that no matter what the future held, no matter what choice she made, her life was already tied to his. But she needed to be sure. "I need to talk to Maryanne first."

Understanding that her family came first, he nodded. "Agent Ardell can take you back to your cousin. But I need something first."

"What?"

Bo rounded the table and pulled her to her feet. His eyes were turbulent as he gazed down at her. When she did not resist, he pulled her to him. He tipped her chin and lowered his mouth to hers.

He meant to keep the kiss brief, to take just a small taste of what had been missing in his life these past months. But Emma wrapped her arms around his neck and pressed her body to his. Her mouth was almost grinding against his as she fought him for the embrace.

All Emma could think was that it had been too long. Some part of her wanted him on every level. But she was also still angry, and between heady kisses, she bit his lip. She thought she tasted blood but didn't care. A part of her wanted to hold back, to punish him for what he had put her through, and yet the other part of her was so relieved he was alive that she wanted to give him all of herself, all he would accept.

Bo pulled back, grasping Emma's shoulders so she would not lose her balance. "Agent Ardell is at the door."

Emma finally realized she could hear a knocking at the door. She blushed because she wasn't sure how long the two of them had been standing there kissing while the agent knocked. "I'll get dressed."

Bo let her go and answered the door. Twenty minutes later, he bid Emma goodbye. The baser part of him wanted to grab her, drag her back inside, and lock the door. The saner part of him knew he had to let her go. She needed time to sort out her feelings, the same as he had. She had only known he was alive for less than forty-eight hours. He could wait.

* * *

Emma left her newly purchased items in the SUV. She let Agent Ardell escort her inside so she could talk to her cousin. Seeing Bryan awake and in the playpen, she went and picked up her youngest cousin. She cuddled the baby, savoring the feel of him.

"I wasn't sure when you'd be back." Maryanne came into the living room, smiling at her cousin.

"Agent Ardell and I went shopping. I picked up some items for you and the children. One of the agents is getting the stuff from the car."

Maryanne took a seat and patted the seat for Emma to join her. "How did it go with you-know-who?"

Emma saw the agent bringing in the bag and waited until he had finished bringing the stuff in before she answered. "Okay, I guess. I don't know what to think."

"Did you sleep with him?"

Trust Maryanne to cut to the chase. "Not in the way you mean. I did climb into bed with him, but we just slept. I didn't want to sleep alone."

"It's no wonder. You could have been killed. I would never have forgiven myself if something had happened to you. You don't know Ping like I do. He could have raped and killed you, and the FBI couldn't have stopped him."

Emma handed Bryan to Maryanne. "It wouldn't have been your fault. But nothing happened. I was just scared. And you-know-who saved me. Believe me, it went a long way toward forgiving him. He risked exposure to save me."

Maryanne put a now-dozing Bryan back in the playpen. "We need to talk."

Emma rubbed her damp hands on her jeans. The fact that they were maternity was still a bit disconcerting. "I know. Did Jonas say anything else to you? Are you still being put into witness protection?"

Maryanne went to the bedroom and closed the door. "Fan is napping. She's tired. She's confused and scared. Leon has been a godsend with her, making her laugh and not focusing on all the bad stuff going on around her."

Emma wasn't sure when Agent Tanner became Leon to her cousin, but she figured it was a good sign. "He cares about you. All of you."

Maryanne dropped back on the sofa. "Perhaps too much. We're going to get our new identities, but Leon wants the three of us to come and stay with him."

Emma couldn't say she was surprised. "What did you say?"

"I stared at him dumbly for a few minutes. Then I asked why."

Emma scooted closer. "And what did he say?"

Maryanne wiped a few stray tears from her eyes. "He

said getting shot last year has put a lot of things into perspective for him. He says he was taking life for granted. But he says now he doesn't. He says he fell in love with me and the children. He says he won't rush me or ask me to make him promises I can't keep, but wants me to give him a chance."

"But?"

"I don't want to use him. I'm a single mother of two, with no job and no past. I thought I would go back to China and raise Fan and Bryan. But Leon is offering me something permanent. But what if I can't love him back? What if we stay with him, and I hurt him? After all he's done for us, he deserves better. But I don't want to say no."

Emma felt her own eyes sting. She didn't want to be separated from her cousin but knew that in this she couldn't be a third wheel. And though her cousin might not be able to admit it yet, she did care for Agent Tanner. She had seen them sit and talk, had seen longing in her cousin's eyes. Maryanne wanted and needed some stability, and though Agent Tanner was an FBI agent, Emma was sure he could give her cousin those things.

Maryanne scrubbed the tears away. "No more of this. I'm tired of crying. I am going to go with him, Emma. Agent Cole has the cover all ready. I'm a widow with two children. Legally I will be listed as both Fan and Bryan's birth mother. And there's no reason you can't live nearby. And I can be there when the baby is born."

Emma smiled at her cousin. "You have your life back. And you have your own baby to worry about. I'm happy for you, and I know that given time, you'll know what you want when it comes to Agent Tanner. Just don't force it or do anything you're not ready to do. He's the patient type."

"And what of you-know-who? He does not strike me as the patient type. What did he say to you?"

"He said he wanted to tie my life to his." Emma recalled the fierce look in his eyes when he said it. But unlike Tanner, Emma wasn't sure Bo really knew what he wanted. He was much like Maryanne; he had no home and no past. And now he found himself with a pregnant ex-lover on his hands. Or perhaps a one-night stand, though Emma liked to think that had the FBI not shown up at her home, it would have been more than one night.

"What are you going to do?"

Emma looked over at Bryan. "I don't have much choice. I don't have a home anymore. I don't have a job or any place to go. And for better or for worse, the child is his. I owe it to this child to see what happens. Part of me knows how much he's lost during his life, even if he doesn't. I guess I want to give him what he's never had before. A family."

Maryanne looked where Emma was. "You still love him. You might as well admit it. Even when you thought the worst of him. I can't say I'm happy for you; he's still a dangerous man."

Dangerous? Yes, Bo was that and more. Emma wouldn't tell her cousin the things Bo had told her last night. It would only distress her. But thinking about Bo's father and all the horrid things he'd done, it was difficult knowing she was carrying that crazed man's grandchild. But Bo's character was stronger than his father's. He eventually stood up to him, did everything he could to balance the scales. She could only applaud him for it. And like her cousin said, she was in love with the man.

* * *

Emma stayed the rest of the week with her cousin as they all prepared to move. Maryanne and the children's identities were all in place, and Agent Tanner was impatient to take them home. Jonas had come around more than once to see how they all were faring. During those visits, he made it a point not to discuss Bo or what Emma's immediate plans were regarding his brother. She supposed he understood her reluctance to make a decision either way. But the time was coming when she would have to choose.

Emma fixed herself a cup of decaf tea, hoping the chamomile would soothe her. Maryanne and the children were in bed, but Emma found sleep once again eluding her. She heard a soft sound behind her and saw Tanner watching her from the doorway.

"You've been pretty quiet about Maryanne's decision to come with me."

"Want some tea?" Emma turned and leaned back against the counter, ignoring his comment.

"Never was much of a tea drinker."

Emma tightened the sash of her new robe and took a seat at the kitchen table. "I guess there isn't much to say about Maryanne and the children moving in with you. Anyone with eyes can see you have strong feelings for her. I just hope you have the patience to wait. Wooing Maryanne is not going to be easy."

Tanner rubbed a hand over his heart. "She's an amazing woman. Knowing everything she went through and knowing from experience that she's only told me a small part of what she lived through is hard for me. But she loves Fan as if she were her own. She loves that baby though she hates the father. She was ready to pack up two young children, go back to China, and raise them alone. I like to think that I can help ease that burden."

"There is more to it than just you helping her, isn't it? You are not without your own wants and needs."

"Yes. I have my own needs. But getting shot last year changed me. It made me take a good hard look at my own life. I had work. But I had nothing else. I knew I needed something more. And when I met Maryanne, it just clicked. I can wait until it clicks for her."

Emma spoke when he started to walk away. "It will eventually. Click that is. And you are right. Maryanne is strong. So in the end, she'll need you to be stronger."

"Thank you, Emma. And you're welcome anytime. Maryanne said you won't be coming with us."

Emma stared down into her cup of tea. "No, I won't be coming with. Maryanne needs to make her own life with her and her children. She's chosen you to be part of that life. And while I'll miss them all terribly, that's the way it should be."

"You're like her in many ways. Don't underestimate your own strength."

Emma just hoped she was strong enough. "Good night, Agent Tanner."

"Just call me Leon. One day we'll be family."

Emma gave him a genuine smile. "You already are. Good night, Leon."

Emma finished her tea and went to lay down. Jonas would be by in the morning, and Maryanne and the children would be on their way to their new home. Curling up on her side, she contemplated what life might look like one day, her child in her arms. And when she could easily picture Bo's arms around her and that child, she knew she had to take the risk that one day Bo might get the normal life he had dreamed of. But instead of the dark-haired, dark-eyed woman of his past, he would have her and their baby in her place.

Sleep finally came, and she had a peaceful night. The next morning, the house was a flurry of activity. Emma packed up what little she had in a duffle bag, then set about helping pack up all the things for the children. There were blankets, bottles, pacifiers, and toys to pack. Diapers were stowed away in a teddy bear diaper bag; fluffy stuffed animals were tucked safely into small suitcases. Once everything was ready to go, her small bag waiting at her feet, Emma dropped onto the sofa, her eyes a little teary as she watched Maryanne stack everything by the door.

"I'm going to miss you all so much."

Maryanne sat beside her cousin and wrapped an arm around her shoulders. "I couldn't have made it this far without you. You can't know how much I appreciate all you've done for me. I love you, Emma."

Emma laid her head on her cousin's shoulder. "I love you, too. And I love those two children. It seems so strange that a few months ago I was facing the loss of my home. That life seems so long ago. But we have so much to look forward to."

Maryanne patted Emma's knee and rose. "And we're being sentimental fools. It's not like we won't see each other again."

Emma laughed up at her cousin. She supposed they were both being a bit melodramatic. "You're right. You go, make a life with Leon. I'm going to go find out what you-know-who has been up to in my absence."

"If he's smart, he's been pining away for you. I wish you luck with that one. It might take a bit of work to house-train him."

Emma thought about that and knew there might be a grain of truth in Maryanne's somewhat outrageous statement. Emma wasn't sure Bo knew how to be normal, or if that was really what he wanted. He might think normal was something he wanted, but she doubted he really knew what that truly meant. His home was thousands of miles away in a country she couldn't picture. His home was gone now that he was dead. He had no heirs, no one who would have cared about his death, other than what they might gain from it. She knew he had a will, and he had left all of his worldly belongings to people who would do good with what he had. But he had been a police officer and the owner of an international corporation. She couldn't picture him being content with changing diapers, being up in the night soothing a crying child, or living out the rest of his life without the excitement and drive he must have lived with throughout his adult life.

Emma was a simple woman who had lived in the country, content to help her father at work while he was alive, then to tend to her garden and sell her flowers. Bo chased bad guys and lived with intrigue all around him. They were from two different countries, two different cultures. And yet, when she was with him, he seemed happy and content.

"Still trying to work it all out?" Jonas found Emma staring into space when he arrived to drive her to where Bo was now living.

"I suppose. I can't help but think that you-know-who is going to be bored out of his mind, with me and without his job, within six months."

Jonas nodded to the agents behind him to start packing up the SUVs. He could hear Fan's giggles from a back room, and it made him smile. "He is in for a big change, no matter what he does or where he goes. Deep inside, where even he dares not look, is a man who's afraid to embrace his future. I'm hoping you give him something to live for. Because Emma, six months from now, if he has no purpose, no one to depend on him, or care about him, I don't know that he has a future. Revenge has been all he's known for so many years. He has had many people, good and bad, looking to him for their livelihood. He has lost all of that, and his mission is almost complete. He's going to need you and that baby to center him, to give him purpose."

Emma once again placed her hands on her belly. "I thought you weren't going to push me."

Jonas shrugged. "I don't need you to tell me that you've decided to try to make it work with him. The shadows are gone from your eyes, and there is an ease about you. You've already made your choice. I want you to know that he does need you now that you've decided you need him."

Jonas held out a hand and helped Emma to her feet. He gave her a brief hug, then grabbed her bag.

Emma said her goodbyes to Maryanne and the children. She had their new address, their new phone number, and their new names safely tucked in her purse. She kissed each one in turn, then let Jonas help her into the SUV. She was suddenly eager to see Bo.

Chapter Sixteen

"Where are we headed?" Emma knew they were headed north and west, but almost an hour later there wasn't much but fields and farms. She could see mountains in the distance to the west, and the view was spectacular.

"Bo surprised the whole family by buying a farm in the middle of nowhere. I believe the town's population might have reached a thousand people in the past couple of years. As far as hiding places go, he picked a sparsely populated place. Not sure it was the smartest move, but he was insistent."

Emma thought about Bo's long black hair and Chinese features. In a small town in rural Virginia, he would stand out. But even if he had the look of Jonas, who you would be hard-pressed to tell had a Chinese mother, he would still stand out. It was impossible not to notice the way he moved, the way he walked, and the way he talked. He was the type one noticed, especially if that one happened to be female.

Jonas glanced over at Emma, but her face was turned away. "We're about five minutes out. He found the property and closed the deal quickly. Not sure how he managed it so fast."

Emma knew. One thing Bo had told her was that he

had a contingency plan. Her guess was that he bought the property for cash. His new name, whatever that might be, would be on the deed.

Emma remained lost in thought until Jonas pulled onto a narrow-paved road. As they drove past a line of trees, a house came into view. The structure was a sprawling single-story home. It looked as if it might have been updated over the years, but the house had an aged feel as if it had been placed on the land many years ago.

Large trees grew in the front yard, a large garage sat off to the side, in the same aged wood. It looked as if the original owners had not wanted to paint the house but had left the wood to age in the Virginia sun. Large windows graced the front, and a covered deck jutted from the side. Far back on the property looked like what might be a working barn and some fenced in area. To the left of the house, not too far beyond the garage, she could see rows of plants, their tender shoots making their way toward the sun. In the distance, the mountains were topped with clouds.

"This is Bo's home?"

Not responding to her whispered question, Jonas patted her hand and undid her seat buckle. He got out of the SUV, stamped his feet to get some circulation back in them, and came around to help Emma out of the vehicle.

Emma let Jonas take her weight as she slid to the ground, her eyes still on the farmhouse. As they stepped closer, she could see trellises on the house with bright flowers climbing them. "There are roses."

Jonas looked at what Emma was staring at. "I guess. I don't know much about plants. I've lived in cities my whole life, or the parts I remember. The only flowers I see are usually fake. Come on. Lian has been helping Bo set up some basics so the two of you will have a place to sleep and eat."

Emma let Jonas take her hand and lead her up to the house. Four steps had to be taken, and the covered porch had to be crossed to get to the front door. She felt nerves jump in her belly, felt her child move in reaction, and told herself to stay calm. This was Bo, not a stranger.

The house opened up into a large living room. The room was bare, leaving the old hardwood floors gleaming dully in the afternoon light. From the entryway, she could see a doorway that led to a kitchen. She heard voices coming from that direction.

"Lian loves hanging out with Bo. She gets worried that her Mandarin will suffer if she only speaks English."

Still holding Jonas's hand, her fingers tightened on his. "You don't speak it, do you?"

Following instinct, he released Emma's hand and put his arm around her waist. "Everything will be okay. I promise."

Emma looked up into Jonas's dark brown eyes. They held warmth and understanding. "Then I guess we should go say hello. I don't think they heard us come in."

Two pairs of eyes met them when they entered the kitchen. The cabinets looked newer, though they looked like they had been custom-made for the house. The stone counters pulled in the warm tones of the wood. The floors were the same original ones from the living room. Lian and Bo were at a large table in the attached dining area.

Bo immediately rose the moment he saw Emma. "Huānyíng huí jiā."

Jonas squeezed Emma's waist before letting her go. "That means 'welcome home.'"

Emma stared at Bo. His once long hair had transformed into a much shorter cut, with the sides cropped closer to his scalp and the top a little longer. A small lock of it fell over his forehead.

"Emma?" Bo came around, concerned that she hadn't moved from her spot in the doorway.

When Bo stood before her, she reached up and touched the lock. "You cut your hair."

Bo took her hand in his. He'd gotten used to the short hair over the past week since he had gotten it done. His free hand brushed it back. "Yes. You should sit."

Lian also rose and went to stand by her husband. Jonas gave her a small smile, letting her know that everything was fine.

Lian took Emma's hand and led her to the chair at the table. "Bo and I have been busy. We've got dinner in the oven. Authentic Chinese. He said he owed you a meal. We just finished setting up your bedroom, too, if you'd like to lie down."

Jonas excused himself to go get Emma's bag from the car.

Emma wanted to cry at the long-remembered promise to make her a meal. She grabbed the first excuse she thought of to leave the room. And in all honesty, it was a real excuse. "Actually, I need the bathroom. The little one likes to sit on my bladder, and the car ride was long."

Bo led Emma to the bathroom. Torn between wanting to take her in his arms or run in the other direction, he went back to the kitchen.

Mirroring Jonas's earlier words to Emma, Lian switched back to Mandarin. "It will be okay. I promise. The two of you just need to get to know one another as who you are now. Emma is going to be a mother, and you need to learn to be comfortable in your own skin."

Bo nodded. He had much respect for his brother's wife. "I do not know how to be a father, or how to be the type of man a woman like her needs."

Lian understood what he meant. Lian could only imagine the things Bo had seen and done. But as far as Lian was concerned, Bo had more than earned a second chance. "Then follow her lead. In her own way, she will show you what she needs."

Bo glanced up when Emma came back into the kitchen. She had taken a moment to brush out her hair and splash some water on her face. Jonas came in behind her.

As far as their first family dinner was concerned, Bo thought it went well, though Emma looked a little strained. Jonas and Lian kept the conversation going. It was getting late when Jonas and Lian took their leave.

Emma watched as the couple drove off. "Why didn't they stay?"

Bo came up behind her. "No spare room yet. Lian set up a bedroom for you, and I put a bed in the second bedroom, but no other rooms are done. I was not sure you would come. But if you did, I wanted to wait so you could make this your home. If I could, I would have given you back all you lost. I can only hope that this helps make up for some of it."

Emma turned and wrapped her arms around Bo. But before Bo could respond, she let him go. She walked into the empty living room. "This is much nicer than my home. But you don't owe me anything. I had already lost everything before you came."

"Had I not come, Jonas would not have shown up. And if Jonas had not shown up, you could at least have taken your belongings. What was left in the house was sold at an auction before the house was sold. And whatever keepsakes and mementos you were able to take with you were lost in the explosion. I know how much they meant to you."

Emma's brows furrowed. Then she got angry. "Bo Lee, you are not responsible for the explosion. You are not responsible for what happened. Ping would have come even if you hadn't. And if you had not come, if Jonas had not come, I don't know what would have happened to Maryanne and the children, or what would have happened to me. And while there might be things that were lost, my family is alive and safe. Ping is out of our lives. Whatever the price we had to pay to make that happen was worth it."

"You are more forgiving than most."

That just made her angrier. "More than who? All those women who were only using you for what you could give them, or the power you wielded? In case you haven't noticed, you're not in Hong Kong anymore."

Bo touched her cheek. "Trust me, I cannot forget. I am as far from Hong Kong as it is for me to get."

Emma's anger faded. He had lost as much as she had, if

not more. But he didn't seem to notice. "For now, let's call a truce. I don't want to spend our first night together fighting. And if it makes you feel better, not everything was lost in the explosion. I have my can of seeds, and I have my family portrait. And Maryanne has a storage unit full of her things and other keepsakes and mementos from before her life with Ping."

Unsure what to do now that they were alone, he remembered what Lian had said about letting Emma show him what she needed. "I will show you your room. You can unpack your things."

Emma followed Bo, confused by his sudden mood change. When he opened a door off the hall of the living room, she peeked into the room. The room definitely had a woman's touch. The curtains were colorful but muted. The area rug in front of the bed would keep the cold off one's feet in the winter. The bed was a king and draped in a solid pale green comforter and matching sheets.

"If you do not like it, we can change it."

Emma looked up at Bo. He had a similar look on his face that he had when she met him. It was that of a man disinterested in the woman standing in front of him. A few months ago, she would have believed that look. She didn't anymore. "Which room is yours?"

He pointed to the bedroom at the end of the long hall at the back of the house. "Right now, it is just a bed."

Emma walked further into the bedroom. To her left was an open door that led to a bathroom. When she opened the curtains, she saw there was a view of the mountains. The room itself was large and would fit a couple of dressers, and the closet on the right was big enough for two. "This is the master bedroom, isn't it?"

"Yes."

"And your room is down the hall?"

"Yes."

Emma turned to look at him, his face still unreadable. "I thought you said you wanted to tie my life to yours."

Bo tucked his hands in his pockets, unsure where she was going with her line of questioning. "I do."

Emma crossed to him and shut the bedroom door behind them. "And you think that tying my life to yours is going to be accomplished by separate bedrooms?"

Bo felt hope flare. "I wanted to give you space. Our relationship, as it was all those months ago, had just begun when it ended."

Emma nodded. He was right. "What is your new name? Jonas told me that he kept my name Emma, but that if it was what I wanted, I could have your last name. He said in China women do not take their husbands' last names, but since we are not in China, I could have your name if I wanted to follow American customs. Legal documents showing we are married can be arranged."

Bo had not wanted to assume that Emma would want to have their new identities married, even if she agreed to come live with him. "I told Jonas to hold finalizing your papers until you were sure what you wanted. My surname is now Hau. On paper, my first name is Jiao."

"Hau. Why that name?"

Bo gestured to the fields that lay beyond. "It translates to 'hay.' Seems fitting given that I met you on a farm."

Emma liked it. "And Jiao?"

Bo sat on the edge of the bed. "That was the name Jonas was given at birth. He felt it fitting that I assume it as part of my new life since he was never able to claim it as his."

"Jiao Hau. I don't know that I can call you that."

"In China, it would be Hau Jiao. Surname is first to honor the family name. But Jonas said that I could just tell people that Bo is my 'American' name."

Emma crossed to where he sat. "It's nice to meet you, Hau Jiao."

Bo would have risen if Emma had not brought herself a step closer.

Emma cupped his cheeks with her palms, the day's growth of his beard rough on her hands. "Emma Hau. Or Hau Emma. It has a nice ring to it."

Bo opened his mouth, but no words formed when Emma kissed him. His hands lifted to her hips, and he held her in place as he devoured her mouth. He was breathing heavily when he pulled away. Emma's mouth was swollen from his. But despite the blood pulsing through his veins, he wanted Emma to be sure. "You can take your time to think about this, to think about the possibility of us."

Emma pushed Bo down on his back and came to stand between his legs. "I thought about you and me when we first met. I thought a lot about you and me when I thought you were a criminal. I thought a lot about you and me when I thought you were dead. And I thought a lot about you and me when I found out you were not dead. I'm tired of thinking. I don't need more time to know what I want. I want my life tied to yours. You said you wanted that, too. So if our marriage is going to be a fictional event, I at least want the rights that come with it. And I want them now."

Bo scooted back on the bed and gently pulled Emma down beside him, making sure she landed on her back and not her belly. His hands shook as he once again claimed her mouth. He pulled his mouth away as his hands found their way under her shirt. "Be sure, Emma. We cannot go back, only forward, if we stay on this path."

"I'm sure."

Bo needed no other words. He lifted her shirt over her head and gazed down at her fuller figure. His heart swelled at the sight of her rounded belly. She would be close to six months pregnant now. There was no denying his baby was rapidly growing inside her.

Emma flushed a bit as he stared down at her body. It was disconcerting to see her body changing, but he didn't seem turned off. In fact, if his body's reaction was any indicator, it turned him on. She reached under her back and undid her bra. As soon as it was unhooked, Bo tugged it away. She closed her eyes as his fingers trailed across her chest, then down her breasts. When he bent his head to her, she held him to her. She had thought she would never feel his touch on her again, and now that her body was so sensitive, she could barely stand it.

"Okay?" Bo pulled back, unsure if the sounds she had been making were from pleasure or from pain.

"Oh, Bo. I missed you so much."

"No more than I do you, Emma."

Emma pulled him back to her, but Bo held himself

back. Instead, he rose so he could strip off her jeans and underwear. He smiled at the elastic drawstring pants.

"Don't you dare laugh. You have no idea how strange it is to fit in your clothes one day and then not the next."

"I would never laugh at you. I can only imagine what it must feel like. And one day perhaps I will be able to take seeing you like this for granted, but not today." Bo stripped his t-shirt over his head and then removed his jeans and underwear. Still unsure if the sounds she had made were pleasure or not, he lay down and then pulled her on top of him so that she straddled him. He could tell she enjoyed the position when she proceeded to rain kisses over his chest.

Emma kissed and laved the skin on his chest, savoring the feel of him. But they had been apart too long, and she didn't want to wait. Her eyes on his, she raised up so she could take him inside her body. She couldn't stop the moan of sheer pleasure at having him inside her again. She felt his chest swell as he took a deep breath, and she could tell he was forcing himself to remain still.

Emma, too, held herself still for a moment, simply savoring the feel of him. She then took his hands and brought them to her breasts. She watched as he stroked her flesh, his large, dark hands contrasting with her pale skin. She began moving on him, holding his hands in place.

Bo remained still, letting her take as much or as little of him as she wanted. Her eyes were closed once again, but he kept his open, wanting to watch her face as she rocked her body. When she convulsed around him, he buried himself inside her as deep as he could go. His hands did not release her breasts until she collapsed on top of him.

Struggling to catch her breath, Emma could feel the sweat of their bodies as she lay on top of him. She felt their child stirring, and she couldn't help but feel as if he or she approved of their reconciliation. But once her breathing was back to normal, she realized that Bo was still hard inside her.

Emma leaned up, leaning her arms on Bo's chest so she could see his face. "Bo?"

Bo felt his eyes sting. "Nǐ shì wǒ de shēng mìng."

Emma saw the dampness in his eyes and felt her own fill. "I don't know what that means, but it sounds nice."

Bo, without separating their bodies, rolled Emma onto her back. "The English translation is 'you are my life.' Emma, I do not know what the future holds for us, but you have honored me by giving me a chance."

Not knowing what to say to that, Emma pulled his mouth down to hers. Bo held his body above hers and began moving slowly inside her. She gasped and tried to pull him closer.

"Let me do this my way. I do not want to hurt you or our child."

She wanted to tell him that he wasn't, couldn't, hurt her, but she lost her voice. His tempered movements had her arms dropping to her sides. The sheets beneath her bunched in her fists, and she lifted herself against him, her movements becoming more urgent as she felt herself tightening around him once more. This time, when she convulsed beneath him, she felt him follow.

Bo dropped his head against her breasts; this time it was he who struggled to catch his breath. He felt her fingers stroking his scalp through his much shorter hair. With one last kiss to her breast, he pulled away and lay beside her.

Emma turned so that she could lie against his side. She smiled when his arm came around her. Unable to keep the words to herself, she tipped her head up so she could see his face. "Bo, how do you say 'I love you' in Mandarin?"

Bo was quiet for a moment, his throat tight. Once he was sure he could get the words out, he spoke. "Wǒ ài nǐ."

Emma rose on her elbow and looked Bo in the eyes. "Wǒ ài nǐ, Bo."

He opened his mouth, but Emma's fingers closed his lips.

"Just let me say it." Emma lay back down and tucked her body back against his.

Bo was silent for a moment. "Good night, Emma."

She smiled and kissed his chest. "Good night."

Chapter Seventeen

Emma found Bo outside in the back garden the next morning. She had slept well, only waking up once in the night to go to the bathroom. A good night, indeed. She stepped out onto the back patio wearing nothing but her terry cloth robe. There were no other houses in view.

"Good morning." Emma stepped into the damp grass, enjoying the feel of it on her toes.

Bo straightened from tending the garden. "Zǎoshang hǎo. You look well-rested."

"I feel well-rested." Emma came closer, curious to see what was planted.

Bo set the small tool down that he had been using to weed the garden. "You would know much more about this than I."

With her experienced eye, Emma could see tomato plants, peas, two different kinds of lettuce, what she thought were radishes, carrots, and possibly potatoes. She could also see some squash and pepper plants. In the back of the garden, some stalks of corn were growing. In the distance, she could see fences and some troughs, but no animals.

Bo took her hand and bent to place a small kiss on her upturned lips. "Come see the rest."

Emma paused. "Let me get my shoes."

Bo watched as Emma hurried into the house and came out a few moments later. She had a pair of slip-on sneakers on her feet but was still in her robe. "Beyond the garden are four sections of fenced land. The previous owner said it was set up so that the sheep could be rotated from each section, so they don't overgraze. Each section leads back to the barn for when they need shelter. There is automatic watering, so you do not have to fill the troughs."

Emma looked over the land and back at the house. She could see solar panels. The garden had an irrigation system. Everything around them was lush and beautiful.

Bo took her hand. "The property was built to be mostly self-sustainable with minimal work. There is a rainwater recovery system that waters all the plants. The solar panels power the home, and the barn has them as well. We are not completely off the grid, but pretty close. Down the path, there are various fruit and nut trees."

"What made you choose this place?" Emma turned her back to him so he couldn't see her eyes.

He ignored her question and instead asked his own. "Do you like it?"

Like it? Emma turned back to him. "This place is amazing. It's so beautiful. But why did you buy it?"

Bo lifted a finger and ran it down her cheek. "I bought it for you. Once you decide on your name, Jonas will get the deed finalized in your new name."

Emma couldn't believe that this was hers. "What do you mean the deed will be finalized in my new name? This is yours."

Bo gently kissed her. "No, Emma, it is yours. If my

name goes on the deed, it might be easier to trace me. How many men with a Chinese surname own property in Virginia? I contemplated a more American name, but that would stand out even more. There is no way I can pass for Caucasian. The deed will have your new maiden name on it. If you choose to go with my new name, it would still be risky to have a Chinese surname on the papers."

"You think Feng is still looking for you?"

Bo nodded. "I am almost certain of it. When Biao was killed, he should have left to go back to Hong Kong. Instead, he is still here, and by here, I mean Virginia. Chatter has been active again. Feng would know that Jonas is my brother. Other than his visit here to bring you, he will not be back until Feng is caught, whether here or in Hong Kong. To be safe, and to protect you and to secure your future should anything happen to me, all that I have is now yours."

"Oh, Bo." Emma's voice was a whisper as she leaned into him.

Bo stroked Emma's hair and placed a kiss on top of her head. "Over to the left is where I think your new greenhouse should go. That part of the land is flat enough and does not have a lot of trees."

Emma pulled away. "I don't want you to do all this for me because you feel guilty."

Bo pulled her back to him. "Guilty? I may feel it, but that is not why I did this. I did this for my child. But mostly I did this for you. In the short time we were together, I knew peace. I knew happiness. Those are things money cannot buy. Whatever I have, whatever I can give you, I will give it. Not because of guilt. I will give it all to you because you love me, because I would not have a future without you. Are those good enough reasons?"

"Yes." Her voice was a whisper. She had held her breath for a moment that he might say he loved her. The words didn't come, but what he said was close enough.

Bo kissed her deeply this time, pulling her body to his. He pulled back when he felt his child moving through the fabric of her robe. Opening it up, he slipped a hand inside. Not saying another word, he scooped her up and took her back to bed.

After Bo made love to her, Emma fell back asleep. When she woke, he was still beside her, his fingers stroking her neck. He had often touched her like this last night, but she didn't think he was aware. And looking up into his face, she could tell he was deep in thought. "What are you thinking?"

Bo tucked her head back to his chest. "Mostly I am thinking that I could never have imagined what life would bring when I came to the U.S."

Emma sat up, pulling the sheet with her to cover her bare body. "You found a brother, a mother, and a sister. It's a lot."

Bo caressed the skin above her breast. "And you. I knew about the other three, though I did not know any of them. I never imagined staying."

Emma held his hand to her heart. "Are you feeling homesick?"

Bo thought about it. "Perhaps in a way. I do not think I will miss Hong Kong and running what was my father's empire. I am not sure I will miss being a police officer either. But I spent a lot of time on the Mainland, and some of that I miss. Thinking about never returning does make me sad. But no more so than you and your home. You lost as much as I have."

Emma couldn't help but feel some of the pain Bo was feeling. She wasn't sure he even realized the pain that was betrayed in his voice. "Except I could at least visit. You can't. I like to think that I gained more than I lost. And this farm is so much more than I had before, and I had no one to share my old home with. I think this will be better."

Bo tossed aside the covers and rose. "I know it will be better. We will make sure of it. I can picture our child growing up on this land, learning to tend it. You will have to teach me how, so I can teach our child."

Emma dropped the sheet and went to the bathroom, her voice calling to him as she went. "No time like the present."

* * *

Emma wiped the sweat from her brow as she knelt in the garden, despite the fact that it was still early morning. She had missed this since she had left home. She loved waking up to the smell of life growing around her. The fruit trees were blossoming, and she could smell their sweet scent as the wind blew. The dirt under her fingernails made her feel like she had come home again. She had easily settled into a routine on the farm in the weeks they had been here.

From her spot in the garden, she could see Bo only a

short distance away. Much as it had been when he first came to her home, he was outside going through what she thought of as his morning exercise routine. He said he needed the time to center himself and get ready for the day. It was strange to see him with short hair, though she still thought him ridiculously attractive. His body glistened with sweat. The fluidity of his body, the flex and play of his muscles, was still a turn on. Of course, she now had the right to touch, and had often, which made her feel more compelled to watch, not less.

Emma took her basket and pulled a few more ripe vegetables. As she did, she saw Bo tense. She stood still as he made his way to her, his eyes gazing toward the long road that connected their farm to the main road.

Emma wiped the dirt from her hands on her already filthy shorts. "What is it?"

Bo took her hand, ignoring the dirt on it. "There is a car on our road."

Emma squinted, but she didn't see one. But as she listened, she could start to make out the faint sound of a car engine. "I take it we're not expecting anyone."

"No. Jonas is still trying to locate Feng. Lian has not heard much since Biao's death, other than bits and pieces. At first, some had been cheering, while others vowed revenge. Nothing came of any of it. Most people thought Biao a traitor, so most were just glad to see he got what he deserved."

Emma leaned into him, but he pulled away. He took the basket from her and took her hand. "What?"

"You're going inside. I want you to wait in the kitchen

until I give you an all clear."

Halfway to the house, Bo's phone buzzed in his pocket. Frowning, he saw it was Lian's number.

Lian didn't give him a chance to answer. She started speaking in a flurry of Mandarin. "Get out of the house now. Feng is coming. He has your mother."

Bo replied in kind, his hand tightening on Emma's as he dragged her to the house. "How do you know this?"

Lian was yelling at the agents nearby to get Jonas. Then she spoke again to him. "I got a phone call from Griffith. He and Naiwen were attacked in their home last night. He just managed to get free and get to a phone. Griffith is on his way to you now, though I doubt, given what I know of this Feng character, that he is in any kind of shape to be driving. Jonas will be on his way as soon as I find him, but it will take time. Bo, please. You need to get you and Emma out. Feng will not hesitate to kill both of you on the spot and then take Naiwen out."

Bo could hear a vehicle getting closer. He reversed direction from the house to the barn. Emma struggled to keep up as he pulled her along, but they managed to get inside and close the door.

Emma, who had not understood a single word of the conversation but could tell something was seriously wrong, stayed quiet while Bo pulled her further into the darkness of the barn. He then opened a stall door.

"You need to stay here. Lian said Feng is on his way. He has my mother."

"Bo." It was all she got out as he closed the stall door and rushed from the barn.

Bo, hoping Emma would obey him, slid around the barn, trying to stay out of sight. Just as he rounded the side farthest from the house, the car he had been hearing stopped in front of the house. Bo watched as Feng opened the door of the expensive sports car. He tamped down his rage as he watched him drag his mother from where she had been tied up in the back seat. Naiwen's face was bruised, and she was hunched over as if she could not stand up straight. He knew only too well the tactics Feng would have used to make his mother talk.

"Let's not play games, Bo. We both know you are here." Feng shoved Naiwen in front of him as he surveyed the land and shouted so he could be heard.

Bo focused on Feng, and not his mother who stood trembling in front of him like a human shield. Little did Feng know that he need not worry. Bo had two guns, each far from reach. One he had in a drawer in the kitchen, and the other in the nightstand by his and Emma's bed.

"Come out, now. Did you think you could play dead? Did you think you could hide from me? I know you too well."

Bo made no noise as he sprinted out of Feng's view from the barn to the back of the house. Feng was on the opposite side and more focused on the house than he was on the dangers that might come from other directions. Bo made his way toward the back of the house, intent on making his way to the kitchen and his weapon, but Feng suddenly reversed direction and headed around the house. Instead, Bo sprinted around the side, hoping Feng would not see him.

"We could have ruled your father's empire side by side. You had it all. And you gave it up for what? Justice? An American dream? You are pathetic, just like your father. I will own all that was his, all that was yours; do you hear me?"

Bo was pretty sure that if he had neighbors, they would hear him. Feng was shouting, his rage palpable as his words rang through the air.

"And a cop! That is unforgivable. I could hardly believe it when Biao told me. But it made sense. There was no other way you could have evaded his trap last year when he set up that bomb for his wife. The only reason you are still alive is because you betrayed your family, betrayed your brothers. I will relish bringing your head back for all to gaze upon the dead traitor."

Bo heard his mother whimper and closed his eyes for a moment. Never had he imagined Feng would use Naiwen against him. He had been so focused on protecting Emma that he had not been thinking straight. And between Jonas and Griffith, he never thought he would have to protect her.

"I will give you to the count of three. Come out, or I will kill her where she stands."

Bo weighed his options. It was possible Feng would simply shoot him the moment he made an appearance. On the other hand, the man was arrogant. But one thing Bo did know was that Feng would not hesitate to kill Naiwen and then hunt him down.

Bo called out from around the house. "I suppose you have been waiting some time for a showdown between us."

Feng held Naiwen still in front of him as he rounded

the side of the house. The look of satisfaction on Feng's face when he saw Bo was unmistakable.

Bo did not betray any of what he was feeling. "It was inevitable. You would never have been content to remain as my number one. I always knew one day you would force a confrontation."

"You are weak. You always were. So yes, here or in Hong Kong, this moment would have come. This was not how I imagined it, but I will still gain the satisfaction of knowing you died by my hand. You did not have the guts to kill your father. You let a woman do it for you."

Bo took a step forward when Feng grabbed Naiwen's hair and yanked her to the ground. He stopped as the gun Feng held pointed at his chest. "It is you who hides behind a woman. You do not have the guts to face me like a man. It is you who are weak."

"Let us prove your theory." Feng cocked the gun he had and pointed it at Naiwen's head.

* * *

Emma could hear Feng shouting from where she hid in the barn. She had no idea what he was saying, but his tone was angry; the words sounded like taunts. From her hiding space, she kept telling herself over and over that Bo could take care of himself. He was a trained police officer and didn't need her coming to his rescue, most likely fumbling his grand plan. She kept picturing every movie she'd watched or book she'd read where the woman, disobeying a direct order, goes fumbling about into the line of fire, getting herself caught by the bad guy.

But knowing she should stay put, and physically doing it, was getting harder as Feng shouted, his voice echoing in the open sky. Bo was alone. And worse, he was barefoot and bare-chested, just having finished his morning exercise routine. She had on sneakers, and while her tank top and shorts didn't leave much to the imagination, she was better dressed than Bo.

Calling herself every name for an idiot she could think of, and wishing she knew how to say it in Mandarin, Emma left the stall and looked for a weapon. She found a long, thick board about the size of a baseball bat. Halting and debating with herself again, she felt her child, Bo's child, move restlessly inside her.

With her free hand, she rubbed her belly. "What do you think? Do we go help your daddy, or do we do the smart thing and stay here?"

The small life kicked at her hand. Emma gave her belly one last rub. "I agree."

Emma used the side barn door to slip outside. Listening, she determined that Feng was around the far side of the house. With the board firmly in her grip, she slowly made her way around the house opposite where she'd heard the voice. It was then she heard Bo's reply. His tone sounded bored, as though the man confronting him was nothing more than a mild nuisance. As she wound around the house closer to the men, she saw Feng's back. Emma took a couple of steps back and saw a petite woman kneeling at his feet in front of him. She could hear the small whimpers the woman made. Emma took one more step back, eased herself behind the man, then ran, swinging the board and making contact with his neck and shoulders.

Bo saw Emma as she came at Feng, but Feng moved just enough so that Emma missed his head by scant inches. Knowing it was now or never, Bo lunged at Feng, taking the man to the ground. As his fist made contact with Feng's jaw, he heard himself shouting at Emma. "Grab Naiwen. Get her safe."

Emma wanted to shout at Bo that she didn't speak Mandarin but got the gist of what he was saying when he shouted Naiwen's name at her. With all her strength, Emma tugged Naiwen to her feet. The woman's arms were bound in front of her, but Emma didn't have anything to cut the binding. Emma simply wrapped her arm around Naiwen's waist and tried to drag her from the scene. She managed to get her to the garden where she had left a pair of pruning shears and a small shovel. Not saying a word, she grabbed the pruning shears and carefully cut the bindings.

Naiwen rubbed her wrists, then grabbed Emma's arm. She spoke slowly to Emma, her English broken. "Feng kill Bo. Help him."

Despite the words being in English, Emma had a hard time understanding her. Though Emma knew the reason for it was more because the woman's mouth was bruised and swollen, not because she couldn't speak the words clearly. Emma kept the shears in her hand and then grabbed the shovel. She pointed to the barn. "Go there. You'll be safe."

Emma didn't wait to see if Naiwen would obey, any more than Bo had waited to see if she would obey him.

Holding her weapons, she raced back to where Bo was. She stopped in her tracks.

Both men were similar in height and build. As Emma watched, she realized they were evenly matched fighters. Both men moved and attacked with the same fluidity. Emma couldn't help but cringe when Feng landed a blow and Bo grunted. As the men circled each other, she knew she wouldn't be able to get close enough to give Bo a weapon. And she doubted either man noticed her; their focus was intense on each other.

Emma took a step back, watching the brutal fight. She heard a loud sound and glanced up to see a helicopter approaching. Torn between watching help arrive and watching Bo, she noticed the helicopter land in the open space where Bo had told her the greenhouse would go. It was Jonas. She raced to him as quickly as she dared, aware now more than ever that she had a child inside her. "They're over there."

Jonas hugged Emma briefly, then let her go. "Go to Lian. Where's Naiwen?"

Emma saw Lian waiting in front of the helicopter, an agent beside her. She looked around for Naiwen. "I told her to go to the barn."

"Something tells me she didn't listen. Stay here. I'll go help Bo."

Lian came forward and hugged Emma to her. "Are you all right?"

"I'm fine. Feng didn't once mention my name. I don't know if he knew there was anyone else here until I slammed a board into his back."

Lian smiled. "That a girl. Now let's go find Naiwen and check on our men."

Naiwen was not hard to find. She stood a few yards behind her two sons. It was not lost on her that this was the first time she had seen them together. Jonas stood at the side, ready to step in should Bo need it. Bo was still solely focused on Feng.

Lian brought Emma to stand on one side of Naiwen, and Lian stood on the other side, with both women supporting her.

Bo was only peripherally aware that his family stood behind him. He and Feng had sparred many times over the years, and both men were equally skilled. Bo knew that he had to remain completely focused, or he would lose the fight. "You can do better."

Feng swung wildly, but then spun and landed a blow. He watched as Bo hit the ground.

Bo barely noticed the grass had even touched his skin when he flipped to his feet, dropped low, and swept his leg out, taking Feng down with him. Feng quickly rolled out of reach and was back on his feet. Bo lunged at him again, this time aiming for his waist. He gripped the man's waist, quickly twisted until his arms went from Feng's wrist to his neck. His hands slid around until he had a tight grip on Feng's neck and arms, immobilizing him in a chokehold.

Feng spit and cursed as Bo's arms tightened. "We could have had it all. But you lose."

Bo's grip slipped a bit when Feng's weight suddenly dropped. He could see that Feng had pulled a small gun out of a holster strapped to his ankle.

Jonas raised his gun to fire at Feng as Feng pulled the gun, pointing it where the women stood. Not knowing or caring who Feng was aiming for, he put himself between Bo and the women. His finger tightened on the trigger, preparing to fire.

But before either man could squeeze off a round, Bo dropped and repositioned his hold on Feng. There was a loud snapping sound before Feng's body dropped where he knelt.

Emma was the first to move. She shoved her way past Jonas to where Bo knelt on the ground. His torso was covered in sweat, his body heaving from the force of his breaths. She went around Feng's body and dropped to her knees. With a soft cry, she pulled him to her.

Bo did not have the strength to move. He couldn't even manage to get his arms around Emma before his entire body sagged against her. He buried his face in her neck, inhaling the sweet scent of her. She moved so that she straddled his knees, and he could feel her tears mingling with the sweat on his chest. When he felt their child stir against him, he found the strength to move, his arms coming around her in a vice grip, afraid someone would take her from him.

Jonas left the couple on the grass, motioning to the agent who had followed Lian and Emma. "Go get an ETA on the ambulance."

Now that the threat had been neutralized, Lian and Jonas helped Naiwen to the house where they could tend to her wounds and give the couple embracing on the grass time alone.

Chapter Eighteen

It was Bo who released Emma first. He kissed her roughly before helping her to her feet. Once she was standing, Bo had to lean on her once again. "I see you do not follow orders any better than Lian or my mother."

Emma gave him a watery laugh, her fingertips going to the cuts and bruises on his face. "I couldn't wait in the barn and let you face him alone."

Bo stilled her fingers. "I am not sure if I should thank you or lecture you for disobeying."

"I've got a better idea. Why don't you kiss me again instead?"

Bo let out a soft oath and grabbed her to him. He knew his mouth was probably bruising hers, but he could not stop himself. He wanted to shake her for disobeying. He wanted to drag her to the grass and make love to her; his fear had been so great that he might lose her if he lost the fight to Feng.

Emma could feel every emotion that went through Bo. All she could do was kiss him back as fiercely as he was kissing her, her tongue dueling with his. It was almost as if he were trying to brand her, and she had nothing but the desire to do so in return.

Bo finally pulled away from her, his breath still

heaving, but this time from desire. His voice was hoarse when he spoke. "We should go check on Naiwen."

Emma wrapped her arm around his waist and helped him walk toward the house. When a vehicle came rushing down the drive, braking harshly near the other vehicles, Bo hastened his steps toward the vehicle.

Emma and Bo watched as a gray-haired man stepped from the SUV. The man looked like he'd been in a fight.

Bo took a step closer to gain the man's attention. "You must have broken every speed record to get here so quickly. Naiwen is inside. She is alive."

Griffith gave Bo a once-over, saw the bruising and swelling on his face and chest, but only gave him a nod as he took the porch steps two at a time.

"Who is that?" Emma watched as the front door slammed open and closed again.

"Naiwen's husband, Griffith. He looks a little chewed up himself."

Before they could make their way inside, an ambulance pulled up. The paramedics quickly went inside, paying no attention to the couple heading their way.

Bo had to rely on Emma to help him up the porch steps, but now that Emma was safe, he wanted to get a good look at his mother.

The woman answered the paramedic's questions in Mandarin, and Griffith translated. Bo kept Emma at his side but came to stand where Jonas and Lian watched Naiwen being examined.

The brothers stood side by side as they watched the paramedics and Griffith hover over their mother. As a precaution, the paramedics wanted Naiwen to come to the hospital. And while Naiwen did not argue, she was not quite ready to be taken away.

Naiwen kept Griffith's hand in hers but motioned with her free one for Emma to come over. The words Naiwen spoke to Emma were in English. "You saved my son."

Emma glanced back at Bo, then at her stomach. "It was purely selfish."

Naiwen smiled and set a hand against Emma's stomach. "This one will have a good life. This one will never know the pain and suffering that the father knew."

Emma placed a hand on top of Naiwen's. "Or the grandmother. Of that, I have no doubt. And once you are out of the hospital, we can get to know one another."

"I am honored to have daughters such as you and Lian."

Jonas clapped his brother on the back. "And the paperwork is official. I just have to get you the documents. You're now a married man."

Emma released Naiwen's hand and went to Bo. She wrapped her arms around him. "I'm glad."

Bo did not say a word; he simply held Emma to him. The two couples followed Naiwen and Griffith to the ambulance. Jonas and Lian agreed they would follow and bring Griffith his car. Bo declared Emma needed to rest. Ignoring the FBI agents outside who were roping off the crime scene and would take care of Feng's body, Bo took Emma to their bedroom. He stripped her and set her between the sheets.

Emma started to protest, but Bo, with just a look, silenced her once again. Though it felt wonderful to be lying down, she was worried about Bo. He had not said much since he'd killed Feng. "Is it really over?"

Bo kept his back to her. "Yes. Jonas will file his report, but one way or another, I will not be named in the official reports that end up being filed. Feng came here alone. Up until the moment he saw my face, I believe he had doubts that I was alive. Otherwise, why would he risk coming alone? His biggest weakness was always his arrogance, and once he saw me, he believed he could take me out. Now that he is gone, anyone who might have cared about Feng is either dead or in Hong Kong. When it becomes known that the American FBI was the one to kill him, there will be a power struggle back home, and someone will take his place. He will be forgotten. He leaves behind no family."

"What will become of the one who takes his place?"

Bo shrugged. "The police will continue to build a case against the new leader and eventually take him down. And then there will be another, and another."

Emma slipped from the bed and grabbed the nightgown she'd left on a nearby chair. She couldn't talk to him while lying naked in bed. She slipped the gown over her head. "You're right. There will always be someone else. But that is not what's bothering you."

Bo tensed when Emma's hand rested on his shoulder. "I was worried about you. I was worried about the baby. I bought this place hoping to leave the past behind and hoping to find that future Jonas was so sure I could have. My mind was so focused on myself that I did not stop to consider that Feng might go after Naiwen."

"She had Griffith to protect her."

Bo turned to face her. "And yet he failed. I have no doubt the guilt of that failure will live with him for the rest of his life. But he is not as young as he once was. Feng was younger and faster. I should have realized what he might do. I knew him better than anyone else."

Emma decided not to play into his guilt. "So fine, you're not perfect. I still love you anyway, and so does your mother. And I might have just met your mother, but knowing what I do, she will not hold it against you. The fact that she was used to try to hurt you, to hurt me, will be eating at her. So why don't you snap out of it and do what you need to do to make what's left of her life and yours what it always should have been."

"And perhaps that is my biggest problem. Why do you love me? Why does she? I promise you I have done nothing to earn it."

Emma closed the distance between them. She kissed a bruise on his chest, then another. "That's the part you don't understand. Love isn't earned, at least not how you mean it. You have to nurture it, help it grow, but it's given freely. You can't coerce it, you can't force it, and you can't beat it into submission. You have spent your whole life at the mercies of other people, and then at the mercy of your own revenge; you can't see that love is simply a gift. And despite what you might think, you deserve it, the same as anyone else."

Bo closed his eyes as Emma placed damp kisses across his chest. "You will never convince me that I deserve you or your love, but I am so grateful to have it."

Emma placed one last kiss on his chest before stepping

back. "Then maybe you'll never take it for granted."

Bo cupped her chin. "Never."

Emma smiled and turned her head to kiss his palm. "Good. Now you should take a bath and soak your muscles. You're going to be sore later. And we need to clean those cuts on your face."

Bo halted her when she would have turned. His eyes never left hers. "I love you, Emma. Always."

Emma came up on her tippy toes and wrapped her arms around Bo's neck. "How about in Mandarin? I like the way it sounds."

Bo kissed her neck. "Wǒ ài nǐ."

Emma giggled at his gruff tone. "Wǒ ài nǐ. Bo, you really should go take that bath now."

He could only agree. His muscles were tightening, and the dried sweat was making his skin itch. He grabbed Emma's hand and took her with him to the bathroom. "You can wash my back."

Emma giggled and wrapped her arms around him once again. "And maybe some other parts too."

* * *

Three and a half months later...

Naiwen nervously held the large bouquet of flowers in her arms. The elevator was not moving fast enough. Griffith was beside her, and he was the only thing helping her stem her impatience. It was not every day a woman became a grandmother.

"If you don't relax, you're going to crush the flowers." Griffith took them from her, but there was a smile on his face. Bo had called them a few hours earlier, saying he had taken Emma to the hospital and that the doctors believed their child would arrive that day. As soon as he saw Naiwen set down the phone with bright tears in her eyes, he knew Bo had called. She rarely cried these days, but when she heard her youngest son's voice, she always cried just a little.

"It is odd. Part of me never expected this day to come."

Griffith bent and gave her a soft kiss. "You probably thought the same thing when Bo was born."

Naiwen's eyes drifted as she thought of the birth of both her sons. "I had such guilt when Jonas was born. I felt like I should have done something to prevent it. His father paid very little attention to him, for which I had been grateful. But when he was born, for a brief moment I forgot all that I had gone through. I forgot about my parents and my siblings. The only thing I could focus on was the little baby I held. For a moment I felt hope. The day I sent him away, I felt that same hope. He became all I could hope he would be and more."

Griffith stepped out of the elevator when the doors opened and pulled Naiwen to the side so they could continue their conversation in private. This was the first time Naiwen had spoken of the birth of her children. "And Bo?"

Naiwen took a seat on the bench Griffith had walked them to. She folded her hands in her lap. "There was no hope when Bo was born. I named him, I kissed him, but I knew that this time Howard would see to it that he was kept from me. My heart broke a little more that day, a heart I would have sworn would never heal. And yet he grew up determined not to be like his father, to be a better man. And though he might have gone astray for a time, he became just as fine a man as Jonas did. I like to think that the part of me inside both of my sons was stronger than what was of Howard."

Griffith set the flowers aside, taking both of Naiwen's hands in his. "I saw your strength the day I met you. You were then, and will always be, stronger than what Howard did to you. You have a light inside that outshone the darkness that surrounded you. And you can be proud of both of your sons. My only regret is that you and I will never be able to have a child together. But what we can have is your grandchildren. So how about we go see your son and await your first grandchild?"

Naiwen kissed Griffith, then kissed him again. There were still moments when she felt fear. There were still times when Griffith had to step back and let her work through flashbacks. But life was wonderful, despite those moments. Griffith was wonderful. And yes, she supposed that not being able to have Griffith's child, a child born of love, would be a regret they would both live with. But she had her sons, and she would spend the rest of her days loving them and praying for the best life for them.

Jonas and Lian met the pair in the waiting room. Jonas came and kissed his mother's cheek. "Emma threw us out. The baby is impatient to come, and she is not in the mood for company. I think she might have learned some swear words in Mandarin. And I'm pretty sure she hurled a couple of them at Bo."

Lian laughed and hugged Naiwen, then Griffith. "Bo is holding up admirably. The doctor said it should be any time now."

An hour later, Emma let everyone back in. She held her little daughter in her arms, with Bo sitting beside her, his arms cradling Emma against him.

Emma gave Naiwen a huge smile when she came through the doors. "Your granddaughter has arrived."

"Yīgè nǚ'ér." Naiwen crossed the room to see her.

Emma held up her daughter so Naiwen could hold her. "What?"

Bo kissed her cheek. "She said 'a daughter.' I think she is surprised."

Naiwen cradled the baby, tucking the blanket away from the small face. She switched to English for Emma's sake. "I had boys. I pictured a boy."

Emma looked up at her husband. "I didn't. I pictured a girl. A girl with Bo's eyes and long black hair. And that was before I got pregnant."

Bo tucked a strand of hair behind Emma's ear. "You never told me that."

Emma kissed him. "It was the first night you were in my home. You were at the table coloring with Fan. I imagined you and me together, and Fan as our daughter. It was a lovely daydream."

Bo kissed her back, his desire for her banked for the moment, but his heart was filled with love for this woman and the child his mother held. "Then I am glad I could fulfill that wish. And any others you might have."

Naiwen kissed her granddaughter and allowed the others to take their turn holding her before the baby was handed back to Bo. "Is your biǎojiě coming?"

Emma took "biǎojiě" to mean cousin. Naiwen often mixed her languages, but Emma was getting pretty good at understanding what she meant. "She and Leon are wrangling the children and will be here later this afternoon. Bryan was sleeping when I called her, and he sleeps so little that Maryanne did not want to wake him."

Naiwen turned to look at her eldest. "You are not getting any younger. When will you give me a grandchild?"

Lian wrapped her arm around Jonas and looked up at him. "Yeah, Jonas, when are you going to give your mother another grandchild?"

Jonas raised his eyebrows at his wife, then gave her a mischievous grin. "We can start on it when we get home if you like."

Lian looked over at Bo, who was still holding his daughter. She gave a heartfelt sigh, her eyes soft as she gazed at the small, dark-haired baby. "I'd like."

* * *

Emma knelt in the garden, tending to some of her newly budding flowers. She had also planted some hibiscus from her stash of seeds, or Bo's China roses, against the back of the house where their bedroom was, and matched the ones out front. By this time next year, there would be the smell of roses in their bedroom as they grew up the trellises Bo had built for her.

From where she knelt, she could see Bo as he played with their daughter. It had taken a little time for them to agree on a name. Emma had considered both American and Chinese names, but Bo had been adamant that their daughter should embrace her heritage and her homeland and insisted on an American name. Emma had compromised. In the end, they had named their daughter Rose Fei Hau. Emma liked Fei, as it was derived from a Chinese phrase given to Chinese children by their parents in the hope that their child would have a bright future.

Emma stood and brushed the dirt off her hands on her shorts. In the distance behind Bo and Rose, Emma could see the large greenhouse Bo had built in honor of Rose's birth. The large, gleaming glass structure had been there the day Bo had brought her and Rose home from the hospital. She had cried a little, but mostly she had stood in awe that he had it built so quickly and had organized it without her knowledge. The structure was perfect, and once her seeds took root and the other plants Emma ordered arrived, she was looking forward to not only planting and cultivating new plants but also to setting up a small play area for Rose and any other future children they might have.

She had worried Bo might find it difficult to settle down in such a remote area. Part of her still did worry. He had grown up in a bustling city and had run an international company while working as an undercover police officer. But Bo seemed more than content to learn how to tend the gardens and talked of maybe getting some sheep or goats to fill the empty pens. She told him to focus on one thing at a time, and he seemed content to tend to the land and his family. He told her that should he get tired of being a farmer, he could always open a martial arts school. Emma had doubts as to the success of such a school in the remote parts of Virginia where they now made their home, but one never knew.

Emma watched with a smile on her face as Bo picked up Rose and headed her way. Her heart still raced when he put all of his focus on her. She tipped her head up for his kiss when he finally stood in front of her.

"Done? Everyone will be arriving soon."

Emma knelt to pick up the tools so she could rinse them before putting them away. "For now. I'm looking forward to having the whole family here."

"Remember you said that." Bo said it without heat. He, too, was looking forward to it. Maryanne, Leon, and the children were planning on spending a few days. Jonas and Lian would only stay the night, as both had to work. Jonas had said they were working on a new case but were mostly dedicating themselves to what Lian called "the baby project." Naiwen and Griffith were also going to stay a couple of days. Naiwen was looking forward to spending some time in the gardens with Emma. Naiwen had spoken of her childhood for the first time in years, remembering the farm she had grown up on fondly, if vaguely.

Emma went in and took a quick shower. By the time she was done and dressed, Naiwen and Griffith had arrived. Smiling as she heard the light conversation and laughter filling her kitchen, she glanced down at the gold wedding band Bo had given her in honor of their "wedding," which consisted of getting a packet of papers legalizing their new identities and then making love on the floor of the living room. Bo had a matching one, though he had taken the time to have hers engraved on the inside of her band. Etched in Chinese letters were the words, "our lives tied together forever."

I hope you enjoyed All Of My Nights! This was book two of my two-book All Of Me series. And in case you missed it, you can pick up Jonas and Lian's story, All Of My Days. Bo is a complex character, one who struggles with his identity. I think many of us have questioned ourselves, our lives, and the paths our lives take us. But Bo is unique in that he didn't think to have a future once his need for revenge was fulfilled. And yet he finds himself in a foreign country with a family he never thought to know, and then finds a woman that he wants but dares not touch for fear of what he would bring into her life. Emma is very much the opposite in that she's very close to her family, and while she is unsure of her future, she looks forward to it instead of turning her back on it. In the end, it is Bo who has to change, who has to learn to embrace life.

You can sign up for my newsletter @ elizabeth-castle.com/contact. Or follow me on Facebook @ facebook.com/elizabethcastle.romanceauthor.

Also, if you enjoyed this book, or any of my other titles, please consider leaving a rating at your favorite retailer, Goodreads and/or Bookbub. And if you have the time, a text review would be lovely. Indie authors rely on readers like you to tell others how much you enjoyed their books.

Happy reading,

Elizabeth Castle

<u>Books by Elizabeth Castle</u>

Single Titles:
 Going Home
 This Kind Of Love
 Chasing Hope
 The Babe & The Librarian (novella)

The Heart's Way Series:
 For Now and Always
 Ask Me To
 Say You Love Me
 Forever Love

Bennett Family Series:
 This Time Love
 A Bride For David (novella)

Contemporary "Retro" Romance Series:
 Loving Jordan

All Of Me Series:
 All Of My Days
 All Of My Nights

Cantwell Quartet Series:
 Falling Slowly
 Unraveled
 Hidden Away
 Entangled

Visit elizabeth-castle.com for newsletter sign up and up-to-date releases.